Virginia Law I

Gentle Hunter

A Biography of

Alice Evans, Bacteriologist

by Virginia Law Burns

ENTERPRISE PRESS, LAINGSBURG, MICHIGAN

LIBRARY of CONGRESS CATALOG CARD NUMBER: 92-73761

ISBN: 0-9604726-5-7

Printed in the United States of America.

To Susan Petersen-Schneider and Douglas Schneider who are a loving confirmation that true friends are gifts from God.

Preface

Choosing Alice Evans as my next creative effort was the easiest decision of my writing career. Everything about her life and times cried out for illumination. When I discovered that no in-depth story had been done about this truly marvelous little lady, I began research that very afternoon.

Now, three years later, I understand what the noted biographer, Leon Edel, meant when he wrote, "... it is as difficult to write a good life as it is to live it."

Gentle Hunter is not historical fiction. Events and their dates, characters and dialogue are as records show them to be. When I tracked down persons who knew Alice, their contributions glowed like unearthed buried treasures. Incidentally, wherever you find a quotation without a source indicated in the text, it will be from Alice's <u>Memoirs</u>.

I especially liked researching those individuals who influenced Alice. Certainly her virtuous, ethical upbringing contributed to her character. She was blessed with a sweet temperament, determination, and a superior intellect. But these qualities alone probably would not have steered her toward the fateful discovery if she hadn't come to the attention of others in a position to guide, advise and assist her. These "others" did, indeed, help her get somewhere. That "somewhere" is a large part of this life story.

Virginia Law Burns
Laingsburg, Michigan
July, 1993

iv

Acknowledgements

Getting started on a new biography always means a phone call to dear friend and archivist, Geneva Wiskemann. Within hours, it seems, a print-out of sources arrives by mail and I'm off. Ilene Schecter, Reference Services Supervisor at the State of Michigan Library in Lansing, is another starter-upper for me. She has an exciting stack of books and periodicals ready when I arrive at that elegant new building. Thanks, also, to Mary Houghton, Reference Librarian there.

Bill Nelton, at the Library Resource Center of the Department of Health in Michigan came to my rescue on a tuberculosis issue. Dr. Carol Scot of Lansing, Michigan, provided vital medical text copy. William Gebhard, microbiologist, and old friend, of Grand Ledge, Michigan, told me of his experiences with Paul de Kruif, and answered my questions about laboratories.

Vital information on pasteurization laws came from Chuck Quasnick, Dairy Specialist, Agriculture Dept., State of Michigan.

Others who helped me with research, were Lois Sabin, John Gleason and Trudy Bower at the East Lansing, Michigan Public Library; Jane Taylor, Extension Associate of the 4-H Foundation at Michigan State University sent information, too.

Wynn Calder and Wendy Thomas of the Schlesinger Library in Cambridge, Massachusetts, sent data on Alice's life to me.

In Pennsylvania, Margaret Green of the Bradford County Historical Society provided me with invaluable primary source materials, including the cassette tape of Alice's interview at Mrs. Green's home; Janice Hicks also traveled, interviewed and dug up facts for me as did June Jennings. I thank Donna Munger, Associate Historian at the William Penn Memorial Museum and Archives for her assistance.

In Bethesda, Maryland, is Dr. Victoria Harden, Director, National Institutes of Health Historical Office, and Curator of the DeWitt Stetten, Jr., Museum of Medical Research, an expert upon whom I leaned heavily for N.I.H. history. She gave me information I didn't know existed. I'm grateful, also to Dr. Leon Jacobs, formerly of the N.I.H., who carefully critiqued the manuscript from a medical standpoint. I'm indebted to Judy Murphy, Deputy Director of the Office of Communications, National Institute of Allergy and Infectious Diseases, and to Jan Lazarus and Elizabeth Tunis at the National Library of Medicine.

Of those who knew Alice, Dr. Alice Cole and Dr. Margaret Pittman dredged up anecdotes and information from their experiences which were available nowhere else. Dr. Pittman, 92 years old, still reports for work at N.I.H.! It is her splendid memory which filled in when I encountered voids regarding early women scientists at N.I.H.

Elaine Engst, Associate Archivist of the Department of Manuscripts and University Archives at Cornell University, supplied key photographs and letters. Dorothy Sponder, National Archivist of the American Association of University Women, put me in touch with significant persons for oral history.

I was delighted to find Elaine Partnow's encyclopedia, The Quotable Woman, Facts on File, N.Y., 1986. Some of the chapter title quotations are from those two volumes.

Finally, my warm-hearted friends, Earl Snodgrass, Maryell Cleary, Ruth Stringer, and Bill Ferguson pored over the manuscript to proof-read and edit. Under Louise Heck-Rabi's superb editorial direction the book grew, and after five revisions, it flowered. I am immensely grateful for her friendship, skill, patience and endurance.

Virginia Law Burns

Chapters

Chapter 1

A Country Girl's Childhood

*"Childhood, whose very
happiness is love."*
-Letitia Landon

"We'll homestead a place and send for you," the sons
and daughters of John and Mary Howell vowed, when they
left Wales in the spring of 1831. The emigrants also left
behind their sister, Catherine, her husband William Evans,
and their several small children.

The settlers quickly staked claims in Pennsylvania's
Warren Township, and being strong and industrious, soon
owned neat, cultivated fields, with good farm buildings
and fences. Other Welsh had been there for almost a
decade, and they had named the hilly, uneven wilderness
land, Neath, after a town in their homeland.

The Howell families in Wales and Pennsylvania kept in
touch by way of letters, which arrived long weeks after they
were posted. Then, in 1833, as spring crept to Wales, slow
and rainy, exciting changes befell the John Howell and the
William Evans families. They left the British Isles behind

them forever, and by the time the wild strawberries ripened in the Pennsylvania meadows, the new immigrants were dismounting from the dusty wagons to embrace their delighted relatives in Neath.

Summer passed swiftly for the reunited and ever-growing Welsh clan. Then – sudden tragedy.

Now the entire village of Neath moved painfully through the woods this crisp October day. Heartsick, the mourners barely noted the wind's sweet dry scent, or sunlight dappling the bright leaves which rustled beneath their well-worn shoes.

John Howell, the patriarch, had died barely four months after stepping off the ship at New York City. The cause of his death was uncertain. Perhaps he caught a disease during the tortuous ocean journey, and overland horse-and-wagon trip from New York. It is certain however, that his was the first burial in the village cemetery, which lay, pristine, two miles northwest from the church.

The coffin rested upon a crudely constructed bier, which the menfolk took turns carrying upon their shoulders. Stumbling on tree roots, the funeral procession circled clumps of bramble bushes, stooped under low-hanging tree branches. All the while, they sang church hymns. The women led; with strong sure voices they carried the melody, and its first harmony. The men blended a high tenor part, and a foundation of sweetly solid bass. They were a moving human pipe organ, perfectly in tune, sorrowing.

They reached a certain hilly, wooded section; carefully lowered the bier to the ground beside a waiting grave. William Evans, who would have a granddaughter named Alice Catherine Evans some fifty years hence, took off his hat.

****

Alice blinked her brown eyes and frowned, straining to recall how the fruit came to be there. Clusters of shiny red currants they were, in a yellow bowl on a table close by her bed. She lay remembering the sharply sweet taste of currant jelly her mother made every summer, and stored in the cool dimness of the fruit cellar.

But now she felt more thirst than hunger. Throwing off the bedsheet, she stretched her arms and noticed that her angry, crimson skin rash had faded. But she flaked and itched everywhere. She arched and lifted herself to straighten the hand stitched cotton nightgown which lay bunched beneath her hip, and winced. Her belly felt like the milk cow had kicked it.

On this July day in 1886 five-year-old Alice Catherine Evans awoke as a survivor of scarlet fever. Her older brother, Morgan, ill at the same time, also recovered from this bacterial disease. Some infants on a neighboring farm died when diphtheria and scarlet fever struck at the same time.

Its medical name is streptococcus pyogenes. It is a social organism, that lives chain-linked together in colonies. Little Alice did not know that this wildly infectious streptococcus, which had nearly killed her, was one of the families of microbes she would work to subdue some thirty years later.

Nor did she know that she would become famous for a discovery which would stun the medical world – a discovery which would save millions of humans and animals from death or a life of misery. Alice Evans would certify that another disease, undulant fever, could be prevented. She would triumph over powerful opponents, and in time, largely because of her steadfast efforts, practices in public health would change; pasteurization of all commercial milk and its products would be required by law. Alice Catherine Evans' superb contributions to medical science would place her among the world's leading medical researchers.

****

NEATH, PENNSYLVANIA 1881-1901

Alice Catherine Evans drew her first breath in the family farmhouse, which nestled among winter-barren hills of northeastern Pennsylvania. This Welsh community, called Neath, endured these frontier days, a settler wrote in her letter to Wales, as "scattered like partridges on the mountains." Alice's mother and father were Welsh; her paternal ancestors had sailed to the United States, because it was a place where one could make both ends meet, and knot them, too.

Tying the survival knots wasn't easy. The folks from Wales, however, worked so hard, lived so frugally, and saved money so steadily, that a preacher once told the Bible Society, "God himself must belong to this laboring class. He was continually working."

Next to survival, Welsh settlers considered religion the most important aspect of their lives. They formed

Congregational, Baptist, and Calvinistic Methodist Churches, whose preachers were self-taught and unpaid. Yet the position held great esteem, for ministers became leaders of their communities. Long remembered in Scranton was a miner who refused a company order to work on Saturday afternoons. "That time," he said firmly, "is for preparing my lesson plans for Sunday School."

Stirring events in the United States, in the year 1881, marked Alice's first months of life. As she dozed in her handmade cradle, the ingenious Thomas Edison hardly slept at all in his drive to perfect the light bulb. Nurse Clara Barton, "Angel of the Battlefield", founded the American Red Cross, and served honorably as its first President. Telephone inventors, Alexander Graham Bell and Elisha Gray, formed the telephone company that Bell named after himself. And Belle Star (born Myra Belle Shirley), infamous female cattle rustler, sheltered Jesse James, even though posters announced a hefty reward for his arrest.

Alice's mother, Anne, bustling about in a long woolen skirt and high-necked blouse, worked long hours, too. Morgan, the Evans' son, ever on the move and asking questions, was about two years old when his sister joined the household.

By the time Alice learned to crawl, our country was mourning the gunshot death of President Garfield. People with enough money to buy books were reading work by the popular novelist and American Indian Advocate, Helen Hunt Jackson. Teddy Roosevelt, a rising politician, ridiculed Mrs. Jackson, saying she was "one of those foolish sentimentalists."

The 1880's was the time that Wendell Phillips, a lawyer, worked for women's rights. "A woman's place in society marks the level of civilization," he wrote.

If Phillips could have leaped ahead in time, he would have seen that Alice eventually rose to an honored professional position in a Washington, D.C. government medical research laboratory. She was to venture, in her own words, into the realm of the "unbelievable, with findings of a nature that could hardly be acceptable." She realized her work would meet with skepticism, or worse, be ignored. Early twentieth century scientists, medical men especially, did not take women's work or opinions seriously.

Alice spent her childhood as a well-loved daughter, safe in the knowledge that she was as highly regarded as a son within the family. The Welsh traditionally placed heavy emphasis upon education. Welsh parents, both in Wales and the United States, sacrificed and scrimped to finance high-quality instruction for their families. They dreamed of sending their children to fine schools for education that would ensure them a higher place in life than that of their fathers.

If this were not possible, pennies saved in little leather purses paid for private vocal and instrumental music lessons, books of classical literature, and tutoring in foreign languages. Families mentored each other. A common sight in Welsh society was the working class – merchants, farmers, miners, craftsmen – spending its free time, not in play or relaxation, but in study.

And how they loved to be part of a debate society! Welsh forensics thrived in the United States, from 1875 to 1915, especially at the height of the great festival, eisteddfod.

At ages five and six, Alice did not attend school. Instead she took informal lessons from her parents. When they did enroll her, she and Morgan cut across the fields by the Bert Jones' farm to reach the one-room Neath School. Alice was a small child; even the presence of an older brother did not diminish the dangers of the long trek to the old wooden building through deep snow and breath-taking cold. Extreme weather conditions, even when she and Morgan were older, often kept them home.

Both children, however, easily made up missed work, and Alice took comfort in having a cousin, Helen Davies, for her first teacher.

Decades later, in a congratulatory letter to her friends who were planning a centennial celebration of the Old Church in Neath, Alice wrote:

"... The school, located north of the cemetery, was filled with pupils. There must have been fifty or sixty of us some terms. When the pupils were most numerous, we were taught by two teachers, but much of the time one teacher taught all grades. My memories of Gertrude Howell and Carrie Upham, are filled with respect, admiration, and affection. Somehow, with that crowd of children of mixed ages, they maintained order and instilled into us the fundamentals of an education. By contrast, I remember the year when a man from outside of Neath taught the school. What pranks we played on him! ..."

On nights when the Christian Endeavor Group met, some of the older students waited at the school until they saw a lantern begin to glow inside the close-by Old Church. Working fast, they banked the fire in the big coal stove and extinguished the schoolroom light. After pulling the heavy door tight, they hustled across the street. This strategy saved the youngsters a long walk home and back.

With her heavy, dark brown hair braided into pigtails,

Alice grew toward adolescence on the Bradford County land her grandparents had cleared. She did her chores carefully, without protest and learned thrift and frugality by necessity. If harsh winters restricted outdoor fun, in the warm months Alice and Morgan roamed freely through the field and hills which surrounded the large, sturdy farmhouse.

Sturdy, too, was this wiry pair of dark-haired children who had lived through a nearly-fatal siege of scarlet fever. They regained their strength. They played hide-and-seek; under the porch was a dim but perfect hiding place. Some mornings they played Mother-May-I? on the wide front steps, before a summer sun could beat down too hot upon them. They scrambled on and about the friendly limbs of the backyard apple tree. When neighbor children or the Evans' cousins visited, Mother Anne let them spread a quilt in the tree's grassy shade for a picnic of fresh-baked bread and meat, milk and molasses cookies.

On rainy days, if it weren't too damp and cool, Alice and Morgan could amuse themselves on the wrap-around verandah-type porch. Nearby, the large pink and white flowers of the peony bush drooped, heavy with raindrops; petals lay scattered on the ground below the trellised climbing rose. Safe and dry, the children played with hand-made toys. They guessed at word games, or read. Especially pleasant, Alice felt, were the times her mother brought her needlework and joined them on the porch. If bad weather persisted Alice's father would do the vital farm work and then carry out another dining room chair. He'd also have a book from his small precious library, or a newspaper under his arm. Often he would begin a discussion about religion, politics, or economics. Alice, listening, sometimes contributing, would gaze over the verandah railing, across the wide lawn, to the dirt road. She wished these times would last forever.

Alice, of course, accompanied her family to the little Congregational Church. There, as well as at home she heard the melodious strains of the Welsh language, and music. Later, she wrote:

... "My connections with the building of the church are rather close, for my grandparents, William and Catherine Evans, were active participants in the life of the community in 1848, and the memory of my father, William Howell Evans, went back to the time of the building of the church and earlier. My own memories go back as far as the 1880's... Neath was a self-contained community then, necessarily so, for the slow transportation by horse and buggy did not encourage the intermingling of neighboring communities."
She went on to tell of a particular joy.

..."On Saturday nights, we went to singing school, held in the Old Church, [Welsh Meeting House] with John Thomas, and later, Theophilis Farnalls as teacher. The singing school was another source of pleasure, as well as education. I remember how thrilled I used to be with the special music prepared for the Christmas and Easter services..."

As she grew up, an obedient daughter, Alice nonetheless marked the fact that men, not women, had career choices. Where would she fit, this petite, shy female, who brought home outstanding grades from the district school?

Love of learning came early in her life, from family and neighbors, who clustered in the Evans' kitchen, or at their big dining table. Alice and Morgan frequently heard talk of politics and economics, subjects uncommon in most rural homes of the day. Their father, William, had fought in the "Great Rebellion", the Civil War, as a volunteer in Pennsylvania's 104th Division. He worked as a surveyor and a farmer. He studied at Marietta College in Ohio, and became a schoolmaster in Neath in the 1870's. Somehow, the nickname "Professor" stuck to him. His older brother, Evan W. Evans, in fact, earned the title as the first appointed instructor of mathematics at Cornell University. Alice would some day learn more about her famous uncle in a surprising turn of events.

Chapter 2

Preparing To Escape

*"If you play basketball, you will
have to stand the consequences."*
- Elderly Male Physician

In Alice's eleventh year, while she attended the district school, enjoyed the long summer vacation with its family picnics and singing festivals, a family tragedy, rooted in illness, was unfolding in Galesburg, Illinois.

The family was that of Carl Sandburg, who would grow up to be our country's grand poet. Alice and Carl never met each other, but they had a common bond. Alice would become an outstanding scientist in the study of infectious diseases. Carl would learn, first hand, about the terrible consequences of contagious disease.

The 15-year-old son of a Swedish immigrant, Carl worked on his milk route with a horse and wagon. He saw diphtheria signs tacked on his customers' houses. The signs meant that people inside were isolated until they healed.

When Carl got a swollen and sore throat, he had to take to his bed. On the third day he dragged himself up and worked. Soon he and three brothers became so ill they could not swallow. Finally a doctor visited. Diphtheria!

Carl reported for work the next day anyway, fearing that his boss might fire him. He did explain that his brothers had diphtheria, but when his employer said nothing, Carl, relieved, but still unwell himself, trudged the milk route.

Suddenly his two little brothers died within two hours of each other. Although grieving and sick, Carl allowed himself only 48 hours off. As a son of a blacksmith, he learned very early that every penny earned was a penny spent for necessities.

Today, Carl Sandburg's poetry, biographies, and ballads of middle America greatly enrich our country's culture, especially those about the laborer, farmer and rancher. Sandburg said he revelled in the lives of women and men, ragged with troubles, yet going on, anyway, to laugh and love in spite of it all. He was a realist, as was Alice. Both were children of immigrants; both left a legacy of hope and strength to their country.

The year 1896 arrived. Alice graduated from eighth grade, marked time, and worked at home for two years, because the district had no high school. Apparently whatever education money the Evans put aside was being used for Morgan. He had moved to the little town of Towanda, Pennsylvania, where the low hills rolled into one another, and students walked to Lake Pond for picnics and boating. Morgan graduated from Towanda High School and Susquehanna Collegiate Institute. He, too, waited and worked before his enrollment at Cornell University when he was 23 years old.

Alice could have been left on the farm until she chose to marry, or remain a "spinster." Instead, the Evanses gave her a chance to prepare for her destiny. Her mother, who had immigrated to Wilkes-Barre, Pennsylvania, as a 14-year-old orphan, had not been given this chance. Anne, the good Welsh mother, wanting the best for her two children, sold sewing machines. They needed the commission money to add to the farm's cash crops. Two students requiring tuition and lodging meant a financial struggle for all.

When an excited, apprehensive Alice enrolled in the Susquehanna Collegiate Institute, it had trained more than a thousand teachers. Most of these women returned to one-room schools, much like those they themselves had attended. By the time Alice graduated, local school districts were starting to tax citizens in order to build high schools, giving all youngsters a chance at free secondary education.

In her memoirs, Alice wrote little about her scholastic experience at the institute. She probably found the studies too easy. What did fascinate her turned up halfway through her three-year course. She joined the newly-formed women's basketball team, organized by one of her teachers. All the players knew it was considered unladylike, and townspeople were shocked, but the team practiced diligently anyway. The women stepped into baggy bloomers made of wool flannel, topped with black sweaters, thickly knitted, long-sleeved, and turtle-necked. The letters, S.C.I., blazed in red across their chests. They pulled on black stockings and high-topped shoes with rubber soles. Instantly, the players steamed in the oppressive uniforms. Modest as the outfits would look today, disapproving conservatives shook their heads and wondered why nice girls would show their legs and parade themselves so!

Alice played forward on the second team, an assignment that must have kept her hopping because of her short height. She sat on the bench as a substitute guard on the first team.

In the 1960's when she was capturing her memories on paper, she wrote:

"One day, in catching the ball, a joint of the little finger of my left hand was slightly dislocated. It was painful, and I went to an elderly doctor to have it set. He refused to do anything about it, saying, 'If you play basketball, you will have to stand the consequences.'

"When the initial pain subsided," she continued, "the out-of-the-way joint gave me no more trouble, but it is still slightly dislocated, a reminder that if someone oversteps conformity, one is apt to have to pay a price."

What an augury this was to be in Alice's career as

a research scientist! The delicate-appearing young woman with the high cheekbones and small, sensitive mouth, began to see, with a heaviness that curled itself around her heart, that life could be cruel.

"Dreams of going to college were shattered by lack of means," Alice said. "Teaching was almost the only profession open to a woman, I had no thought of doing anything else."

So Alice's spirit, clamoring to emerge, nudged her into basketball, with its fast-paced aggression. A short step toward social rebellion, but a definite one. Before gametime, in the locker room, her teammates chattering, Alice pinned a large bow more securely to her mass of upswept hair, then ran to the playing court. A tiny person who quickly learned ball-handling strategies, Alice always gave the game her best shot.

Alice graduated from the school in Towanda as one of the last class before its closing. In a recorded interview, she laughingly remarked that she wasn't sure whether or not she had something to do with the demise of the school.

Loading her bags into the back of the Evans' buggy on a June day in 1901, Alice rode the 50 dusty miles home to Neath. Back to her girlhood room and the very school she attended as a child...this time as a teacher.

NEATH, 1902-1905

Alice knew little of the township's school history. Her ancestors had arrived many years after the first school in the settlement rose out of the woods in the early 1800's. It was a school in which logs had formed the walls and roof with ash tree bark laid over the whole structure. On its floor of basswood slabs generations of teachers and students had walked. They shared benches and saw only daylight through the greased paper windows.

Pupils who lived close to the Van Gilder farm, studied in what had been a sawmill. Nearby this converted building lay a huge rock. When the winds breathed warmly, and the sun glowed just right, the children begged teacher to hold class outdoors. What joy they felt as they dashed about, dragging tree limbs and brush, to weave a bower over the rock for teacher's protection! How the enchantment held as they sank to the meadow grass, cross-legged in the dappled shade, precious readers or slates in their laps. Maybe teacher would read them a story!

Almost a hundred years later, Alice dipped a steady pen into ink, and signed an annual contract, four successive years, to teach. Her classroom had desks and glassed windows, and the walls were of milled wood.

Harvest-time came, with its overflow of carefully-tended garden vegetables, which Alice's mother prepared for the dinner and supper meals. Carrots, turnips, cabbages, and parsnips went to the root cellar, where they lay buried in sand for use during the winter. William, Anne, and Alice enjoyed the vegetables slow-cooked, in stout mutton and beef stews. The teapot was always at hand, along with the loaf of bread and butter, for the Welsh ate often, and consumed hearty snacks between trips to the dining table.

****

Examination week! Alice eyed the piles of test papers, and the grade book filled with names and percentage marks. These days trailed a damp spring, and Alice sat, weary-worn, at her teaching table, remembering the friends and teammates in Towanda she had said good-by to barely a year ago. Could there be more to life than being back home and working at an acceptable job? It wasn't that she did not appreciate the sacrifices her parents made to educate her. And she truly felt a deep, strong attachment for her birthplace, with its sweetly rounded hills. She needed the solitude of woodland strolls, when she gathered wild ginger and sugary wintergreen berries.

Yet her feelings, Alice concluded, were less than sweet. Life's vital spark seemed to flicker dimly, and she bided her time, privately restless, during a two-year stint at primary school, where she instructed four grades. (One winter broke the record for coldness – 42 degrees below zero! How the "big boys" struggled to keep the potbellied stove glowing in the drafty, frame schoolhouse!)

Her quick mind craved challenge; desperate for a change, she switched to a neighboring school "... the personalities of the children provided interest," she said later, "but the subject matter became boring as it was repeated year after year. I was glad when I found a way to escape."

How she escaped is our story's real beginning.

Chapter 3

"A New Direction"

*"Is there anything as <u>horrible</u> as
<u>starting</u> on a trip?...the last
moments are earthquake and
convulsion, and the feeling that
you are a snail being pulled off a
rock."*

– Anne Morrow Lindbergh

It began with a rumor. Possibly the information trickled
down from Cornell University through Morgan, who had
been there studying agriculture these past three years. The
rumor became fact. A training course in nature study was
about to be offered, tuition free, to rural schoolteachers. It
would be directed by the School of Agriculture, and could
accept students from out-of-state.

Alice's heart leaped. Here was an opportunity to enhance

her education, to attend a real university at a price she could afford. The campus at Ithaca, New York, would be heaven; a chance to stretch her mind and be near Morgan – at least during his final year at Cornell. Glowing with anticipation, she delved into the details. The curriculum was the dream of Libery Hyde Bailey, Dean of the College of Agriculture at Cornell. He wanted to develop within rural children a love of nature, by training teachers in this field. He believed farm families should enjoy their lives more fully, through an understanding of plants and animals and their place in the world.

Alice withdrew the money she had saved from four years of being "Miss Evans." She would need it for board and room, and other living expenses.

CORNELL UNIVERSITY 1906-1909

Looking back at her early years, Alice wrote in her Memoirs, "Until my academic education was completed, I seemed never to have an opportunity to make a choice in matters concerning my future. I always stepped into the only suitable opening I could see on the horizon ... I always thought that somehow I drifted into the work for which I was best adapted."

Did a guardian angel hover near the shoulder of this unpretentious little woman who was now 25 years old? Was she being given incredibly good luck and direction early on to compensate for conflict she would meet later?

Excited and probably not overly philosophical, Alice settled in at Cornell University. Although hers was but a two-year course, Alice and other young persons joined students who were taking basic agriculture classes. She found herself being taught by "Cornell's distinguished professors, and some who attained distinction later."

This new university, financed and directed by Ezra Cornell, became a leader in democratic organization of curriculum. Ezra had made a fortune after he developed the Western Union Telegraph Company. He wanted to use some of his money to fulfill his vision of departing from the old European university ideals. He said, "I would found an institution where any person can find instruction in any study."

Andrew White, Cornell's first president, spent his professional life striving to fulfill the wealthy man's dream. Alice described him: "When he (White) took a walk, he could be identified at a distance by his white beard, and sometimes by the cloak that he wore occasionally, instead of an overcoat."

Another prominent professor who taught the nature students was Burt G. Wilder. Like Professor White, Wilder had been with the University since its inception. Alice described him as a "legendary character." The subjects he taught – hygiene, comparative anatomy, physiology and vertebrate zoology – led to discussions and demonstrations that surprised the prudish trustees, but didn't raise any eyebrows within the classroom. What was "irresistibly tempting, " Alice said, "... were the animals used in his laboratory." Student practical jokers just couldn't contain themselves.

Yet Dr. Wilder had deep convictions, and ran a tight academic ship. Everyone even slightly associated with him, and some who were not, knew that he hated intercollegiate sports, class spirit, secret societies, smoking, prudery, idleness and foot stamping in classrooms. Alice must have had moments when she wondered if the good professor disliked these activities in any particular order. Since there is nothing in her memoirs suggesting she indulged in any of his peeves, theirs must have been a stable student-professor relationship. But what if she had still been playing basketball?

As Alice dipped joyfully into the kettles of fresh intellectual material, she grew more respectful of the old man's talent and dedication, in spite of his oddness. When she discovered a tie between Professor Wilder and her father's brother, Evan Evans, she felt even warmer toward her teacher. In 1867, the new president of Cornell had written to Evan at his post in Marietta College, and appointed him Cornell's first staff member. That same year, Burt Wilder joined the faculty.

Alice, with modesty expected of young women, did not speak of her relationship to Evan "...because I thought the gap between us was very wide." But when she studied in the library, a frequent and observant patron could expect to see the quiet female student with small regular features and expressive eyes, sitting close by the portrait of Professor Evans.

The delightful custom of early university days – that of encouraging students to work closely with their instructors and meet them socially after hours – charmed Alice. She called John and Anna Botsford Comstock a "beloved" couple, who had worked together in nature study for more than fifty years. Judging by Alice's description of Anna's career, we can see how Anna became a role model for young women. As director and guide of rural school nature study, Anna accomplished her goals early in her life's work. Amazingly, in 1878, the University had awarded her status as an assistant professor.

Anna had broken into a strong, ivy-covered clique where only men were allowed. She did it through devotion and hard work (and the backing of a very vocal professor, Liberty Hyde Bailey.) But the Board of Trustees opposed the promotion and in less than a year, Anna became once more a lecturer.

During her terms at Cornell, Alice often walked to the Comstock home on campus. Along with other students and faculty, she basked in the "generous hospitality" of the grand old couple. She studied under both Anna and John. With relish, Alice wrote about Anna"... she remains on record as the first woman to hold professional rank at Cornell."

Anna Comstock's guiding star, Liberty Hyde Bailey, was Alice's hero, too. He proved to be the most notable educator and scientific genius ever to come out of our country's farm and plant biology schools. He founded the Junior Naturalist Clubs for rural school children. "There is as much culture in the study of beet roots, as in the study of Greek roots," he said. His idea of hands-on learning spread fast; the name changed to Boys and Girls Clubs. In 1914, Congress passed the Smith-Lever Act. It established the Cooperative Extension Service, and not long afterward, the youth program, 4-H, sprang up. "My aim in teaching," Bailey said, "is to open a child's mind by direct observation to a knowledge and love of the common things and experiences in his environment."

Bailey was born in western Michigan. As a youngster, he climbed the sand dunes and studied the woodland under the brilliant botanist, Lucy Millington. Lucy always had time to identify plants he brought to her, listen to tales of his discoveries, and encourage his observations of nature. When he left to attend college she gave him her botany collecting-case. He carried it, a cherished memento, all his life.

With such blessed beginnings, Bailey grew to be a "rugged individualist with tremendous energy for thinking and doing," a colleague said.

Bailey taught at Michigan Agricultural College until 1888, when Cornell made him an irresistible offer, (a compound microscope and a trip to Europe as sweeteners). The University then provided the means to make his dream of bringing nature appreciation to everyone a reality. In 1909, when the nature clubs and extension services began to evolve from his leadership, agricultural research went from campus to farm.

Colorful and unique in his many talents, no one had more sought-after influence than he. A prolific writer, he explored and collected plants world-wide. Even as a young woman, Alice said that studying with him was an "exceptional privilege." She took his course, one designed to look beyond scientific knowledge toward beauty in nature. Alice and others would visit the Baileys on Sunday evenings. There, guests listened comfortably, while the Dean read to them. Once in a while he recited his own poems.

Daily Alice trembled inwardly at finding herself to be a minnow in the ocean of lectures and workshops. She told her family, "I had no way of gauging my own ability against the general run of students, so I worked very hard for fear of not measuring up."

Her housemates fondly called her "The Grind", because, they said, the sliver of light showing under her door at night was always the last to go out.

The two-year nature study course ended. Alice had earned another certificate – one that could be used as a bargaining tool for a higher teaching salary. She realized, with wonder, that the person she had become was very unlike the plain little schoolteacher who had fled the Welsh community. The mental and emotional enrichment Alice gained from those first two years at Cornell had pointed her in a new direction. She now saw a glimmer of a goal – perhaps to seek a career in a man's world. As Alice waveringly focused on this fresh outlook, by chance a seed sprouted.

It cropped up from Cornell's School of Agriculture.

Chapter 4

"The Big Chance"

"You got to get it while you can."
- Janice Joplin

As in a beautiful, recurring dream, Alice verified the college's offer to forego tuition for qualifying students who would agree to study pure science. With new technology, certain sciences were springing ahead in theory, only to find no trained persons to fill research positions.

Alice surprised herself. "When the course in nature study was complete," she said, "I was no longer interested in obtaining the certificate for which I was eligible..."

She needed no prodding to gather her credentials, win the grant, and be transformed into a full-time agricultural student. Her life became vital, dynamic; it shifted into high gear. She shared a rented room at Alumnae House on Eddy Street, a Cornell Alumnae-sponsored home for female students. There, Alice had some 30 sisters, a status which pleased her immensely.

In addition to being drawn into an exquisite intellectual

25

and cultural setting, Alice savored the upcoming two years of being a "real" university student, for, she said, "...my interest in science had been whetted by the basic courses I had taken. Any branch of biology would satisfy me."

Good fortune abounded. She was required to enter a few courses which seemingly did not relate to agriculture. English composition she treasured, and it served Alice well throughout her lifetime. The political economics class and its work sessions brought back delicious memories of discussions around the kitchen table and she thrived on the class debates.

She gladly gave up some of her paying jobs when she won a Roberts scholarship during her junior and senior years. Because of it, ..."I was able to complete the requirements for the degree of B.S. in Agriculture during the two years, " Alice wrote.

Our country's need for scientists coincided exactly with Alice's dawning vision for a career. Cornell University, leading the country in agricultural research at this turn of the century, announced a new policy. Students had to specialize, either in dairying, animal husbandry and the like, or bacteriology. Alice scanned the bulletin's next paragraphs. Yes, there it was! Student majoring in bacteriology would have free tuition! Her spirits soaring, Alice typically understated her feelings when she remarked that it was "perfectly satisfactory."

She would soon learn a great deal about bacteriology as a separate science.

Robert Koch, a German physician, is considered, justly, to be the father of bacteriology. He created the science of bacteriology when he discovered the germ that causes tuberculosis. Louis Pasteur, working in France at the same time, the late 1800's, already had proved that disease is caused by living organisms. He later developed a vaccine to protect humans from rabies. Koch's and Pasteur's revelations were possible only because of the evolution of the microscope. There is strong historical evidence that in the year 1535 the concept of a compound optical magnifier was known and being used as a telescope in Italy.

Compound microscopes most likely were in existence by the year 1590. This microscope had two systems of lenses. One system, the objective lens, magnified the object. The second system was the ocular lens. It magnified the image from the objective lens. From then until the early 1800's, not much happened to improve the compound microscope.

Around the first part of the twentieth century, glass-making methods upgraded dramatically. Glass factories began to produce lenses which gave clear, undistorted images and the power of magnification in compound microscopes seemed miraculous. The exciting world of microscopic plants and animals was conceived and a new branch of knowledge, bacteriology, was born. It opened fantastic vistas to the work of medicine.

Alice entered this new world when she was 27 years old. In this different, science-drenched environment Alice studied dairy bacteriology with Professor W.A. Stocking, and another, more general, course of basic bacteriology from Veranus Moore of the Veterinary College.

Of necessity, Alice reverted to working part-time. She mentioned two sources of income in letters to her parents. One was housework. She did seven hours weekly labor in Alumnae House, (not counting the maintenance of her own quarters). Regarding work for hire, she wrote, "... I have been working quite steadily on catalogs... earned about 12 dollars at that. I am going to Prof. Fippins this afternoon to index some bulletins for him..."

In spite of work commitments, Alice managed to achieve excellent grades. This perfectly-groomed little woman, so quietly reserved, shone in her ability to grasp difficult concepts and carry projects through to completion.

Professor Stocking took particular notice of her. Before Alice's last year ended in Agriculture School, he recommended her for a scholarship in bacteriology.

It was a grant, offered every other year by the University of Wisconsin to graduate students. Alice learned, without alarm, that only men had ever won the award. She would risk rejection. What did she have to lose?

More news from Wisconsin reached Alice about this time. The word was that its College of Agriculture Board was preparing to train an instructor to teach bacteriology to students of domestic science (home economics.) Since these pupils were always female, it occurred to Alice that she might get her small foot in the side door of a university teaching job.

Then another choice turned up. Alice wrote home saying she "... was on campus and went in to talk to Prof. Stocking...about that work next year. He said that the state boards of health are employing a great many women in their laboratories and he thought it a good field."

With her last year in school coming to a close, Alice applied for the Wisconsin graduate grant, keeping her ears tuned for other jobs within reach.

It had not been, however, all labor and no fun. Alice enjoyed various and delightful social occasions in her four years at Cornell. Teas, sing-alongs, and garden parties balanced her days and mellowed the toilsome hours. One winter week brought such happiness to Alice, she penned a longer-than-usual letter home to Neath on a Friday, instead of Sunday. It said, "...Well, this has been one of the gayest weeks I have ever experienced..."

Starting with the previous Tuesday, she mentioned a "little spread" put on for her in the room of a housemate, Louise Auerbach. The following afternoon celebrations began to accelerate.

Let's imagine it is the next day and we are looking in at Alice from the doorway. A fastidious person, she is standing on tiptoe in scuffed but polished, ankle-high shoes peeking at her reflection in a mirror fastened to a walnut chest of drawers.

Yes, she muses, the brown combs are holding my hair in its coil. No time, anyway to redo it. There is the faint tinkle of the dinner bell; as always, her healthy appetite and the aromatic cooking odors wafting up the stairway propel her downstairs. She smiles to herself. Is she remembering the birthday letter from her parents in Neath? Does she reflect, "I'm twenty-seven years old, and it's surely taking me long enough to get ready for a job. Soon, though, I'll be sending out work résumés."

In the dining room the housemother hurried toward her. "Alice, dear, you and Louise will sit at my table tonight. Come along, now."

Alice smiled at Louise, and raised her eyebrows as they tagged after the matron. Sitting down, she noticed a little man of molded butter that lay on a tiny plate by her place setting.

She realized, flushing, that one of the 30 women had made it as recognition of her work in dairy research.

"Louise! Look at my butterman!" Alice said. "How do you suppose he got here?"

But Louise only giggled and shrugged her shoulders. Alice, delighted at the thoughtful surprise, grinned at the bright faces of her housemates, who chattered politely as they passed big platters and bowls of pork chops and cream gravy around the table, but avoided eye contact with her. She wondered if these unusual doings were because of her approaching birthday, but she could think of no sensible way to find out.

After dinner the women gathered in the drawing rooms. Alice savored this hour for it was respite; they exchanged their experiences, they cemented friendships. Sometimes it was the only time of relaxation in her day.

Darkness fell. Her books and laboratory notes nagged at her conscience, yet she lingered. The warmth and cheerfulness of the firelit room and her sisters seemed almost hypnotic.

"Don't break up," Alice called out. "I'm going to pop some corn for everybody."

A quick titter rippled through the rooms. Alice wondered at this as she disappeared into the kitchen.

Returning with huge bowls of popcorn, Alice stopped, mouth agape in astonishment. There, fixed in various theatrical poses was a gorgeous Grecian goddess, Julius Caesar, a Scotsman, a cowboy and two little boys!

"HAPPY BIRTHDAY, ALICE!" The chorus of costumed and conspiring housemates shouted. "Let's play some kid games and forget exams!"

"We can't let this good music go to waste!" another said, moving to a popular tune rollicking from the piano. Everyone danced. They licked stick candy, ate gingerbread animal cookies and fancy nuts.

Then they gave her gifts. Alice unwrapped the little packages carefully, her eyes shining. One lead pencil- "Because you are a grind," said the note. A tiny blue glass oil lamp, "To burn the midnight oil" she read. A small bottle of perfume (Just for being Alice.) She sniffed the scent, applied a generous amount to her wrist and waved her arm in an opera-like flourish. Amid the laughter Alice rose.

"Such a nice surprise!" she said, and her lips trembled as she realized the amount of effort and planning the girls had put into the occasion. "Thank you. I'll never forget this evening."

(Alice was always to remember these happy hours, for her parents kept the letter she wrote to them describing the special week. Many years later they gave it back to her.)

Alice had more exciting times that birthday week. The next night, Thursday, the upper classwomen and graduates of Alumnae House gave a party that was the highlight of the college social set. Alice continued in her letter:

"...We had about a dozen nice young men here. I guess they all had a good time, for they stayed until nearly half-past twelve – horribly late for Ithaca.

"We dressed potatoes and carrots in crepe paper; we made outlines of animals on cheesecloth by sewing on baby ribbon. Of course, the fun of that was seeing the men sew. We danced part of the time. For refreshments, we had ice cream and two kinds of cake, and fruit punch (made of oranges and lemons.)"

She went on to say that the first and second year students in Alumnae House had completed plans for their own party. "...We will have to stay upstairs..." Alice wrote.

Saturday night brought more good times. Alice and her housemates were expected for a visit at Mrs. Kerr's place. Mrs. Kerr apparently had been housemother for Alice's brother, Morgan, when he attended the College of Agriculture. (Morgan graduated from Cornell in 1906). Alice made this mention particularly for him.

To cap off the glorious week, Alice anticipated seeing May Upham, a hometown friend, who would be arriving to spend Saturday night.

In contrast, toward the end of her letter, Alice wrote of a fraternity house blaze, saying that she heard "...It was quite a serious fire." Her last paragraph responds to her parent's letter, delivered that very morning. Referring to their search for a smaller house in town, Alice said "...it would be nice to have near neighbors and have mail so handy..."

William Evans was then 71; Annie was 62. The large isolated farm was surely a burden. (The oldsters did move and some 20 years later, their homestead burned to the foundation.)

Alice closed her letter, writing "...Please forward this letter to Morgan: it would be too much to write all over again." Morgan lived at that time, in Wooster, Ohio, employed by the State College as plant breeder.

Winter melted into spring; Alice waited and wondered as the days passed. When would she hear from the scholarship committee? She hoped Prof. Stocking had given a kindly description of her abilities. He had been fatherly and supportive but she wondered if he would champion her in an area where women did not tread.

Her anxiety ended the day she learned that she had been chosen to receive the scholarship. With it she had breached the thick walls of male tradition – all on the strength of her own skill and Prof. Stocking's faith. Within weeks, Alice and a proud Prof. Stocking had pulled together everything necessary for her graduation from Cornell, as well as preparations for going away to Wisconsin. Worries about seeking a full-time position faded, at least for the coming year.

Alice carefully packed her modest wardrobe and books. Saying good-by to Alumnae House girls wrenched at her heart. They hugged, dabbed at tears and promised to write to one another. Carefully packed in her bag was The Cornell Class Book. The caption next to her portrait mentioned that Alice had been president of the Girls' Agricultural Club during her senior year and that she was ..."Steadfast in work and friendship. She is of the sort who succeeds..."

UNIVERSITY OF WISCONSIN

Madison, 1909-1910

On the train, Alice's first long journey, she had 750 miles in which to ponder her future. Her emotions peaked and ebbed as she considered her first job in the "real world" and dipped, at the next breath, into melancholy when she realized how much she would miss her friends and housemates. Would a midwestern university be greatly different from eastern schools? What would graduate study be like? Alice, while appearing young and fragile, was 28 years old and hardy. If she felt fatigue now from her past school and work loads, she knew it would pass. Resting her head on the upholstered train seat, she hoped her money would take her through the year.

Professor Hastings, she knew, was to be her advisor. Arriving in his university office in Madison, she sat very straight, and studied the professor shyly from the edges of her eyes. He seemed pleasant.

"I see you have a good background in biology," he said, shuffling through Alice's records.

She nodded and smiled.

"May I suggest you strengthen your knowledge of chemistry?"

Alice's eyes widened and she clasped her hands in her lap. The idea had not occurred to her.

"Thus," Alice wrote later, "although I held a scholarship in bacteriology, I spent two-thirds of my time studying chemistry."

In so doing she would quickly discover herself privy to a series of experiments which led to an exciting breakthrough in human nutrition – one with world-wide benefits.

Alice studied the chemistry of nutrition under Dr. Elmer McCollum. He became one of her favorite teachers, and remained a friend all her life. As one of only four graduate students, Alice looked forward to his lectures. She doted on his laboratory sessions. He taught, she said, "...explaining any point which he thought might not be entirely clear. Often, his teaching was in conversation with individual students."

McCollum had another side – that of researcher. He was conducting experiments which led to the discovery of Vitamin A some three years later. Alice said she heard "much about 'Fat Soluble A' and 'Water Soluble B'" during her classes with the doctor. McCollum is credited with giving vitamins their letter system in 1915. (The term "vitamine", later changed to "vitamin", was suggested by a Polish scientist, Casimir Funk).

One day Dr. McCollum mentioned that his experiments were becoming "so demanding of concentrated thought, that he could not stop thinking of the problems at night." He seemed to be driven, this fledgling scientist, by the task he had set for himself. Insomnia plagued him. The pressure of endless hours in the research laboratory showed in the classroom. He happened to glance at Alice just as she turned back to a page in her notebook searching for a previous entry. McCollum ceased speaking, and staring pointedly at her, said, "I will proceed when I have everyone's attention."

Writing to her nearly a half-century later, the professor most likely had no memory of this incident. He did recall her "friendliness and engaging smile."

One can only guess how much his work affected his social life, if indeed he had one, but the youthful researcher went on to win acclaim for his work. He was the first to study the effect of Vitamin D on bone formation. Too, he brought to light the fact that calcium and magnesium are minerals important to the human diet.

Alice, the student, could not yet comprehend McCollum's stress. The time would come, however, when Alice the bacteriologist, the researcher, would understand perfectly.

When the last semester ended, and Alice had in hand her Master of Science Degree, she took a big breath and let it out slowly. She felt she could sleep, non-stop, for a week. She did not hesitate when Dr. McCollum asked her to stay in Madison to pursue a doctor's degree in bacteriology. "I believe I can obtain a fellowship for you in chemistry," he urged.

Chapter 5

A Finish and A Start

> *"So I never lose an opportunity of
> urging a practical beginning,
> however small..."*
> – Florence Nightingale

Wearily, Alice shook her head.

"I'm sorry, Dr. McCollum. I realize you could be presenting me with a great opportunity. But these past years have been a financial drain – a physical drain, too. I want relief. "Besides," she said, with a sweet-tempered smile, "I don't consider myself so well prepared for chemistry as bacteriology."

No one could foresee, of course, how prophetic her decision, her very words would be. True, she needed respite. But she also understood which doors were locked to women in science. How important would a doctorate degree be in her future? Two of her favorite teachers, Professors Stocking and Hastings, had climbed to the top of the scientific ladder without advanced degrees.

As Alice trailed back to her room from McCollum's office, she told herself that now she had time to read history and literature. She could listen to classical music; touch the various arts she had yearned for. Maybe, sometime I'll return to academics, she thought. Yet she did not go back to school, full time, ever again. The "why" of it began with a choice Alice made.

On her desk lay the precious vellum document proclaiming that Alice Catherine Evans had completed requirements for a Master of Science Degree in Bacteriology. Alice fingered the diploma absently and reflected on her future – a small, gentle-faced farm girl about to enter the work force. But where?

In 1910 she was a rarity – a woman scientist. If she had anxious moments, she was being human. What, she thought, if jobs in labor and the professions continue to be dominated by men? Would she end up, dispirited, listening to glassy-eyed schoolchildren recite multiplication tables? Society already looked upon her, at 29 years old, as an old maid who defied convention. After all, hadn't she chosen a career which ordinary women and men did not understand?

Still, Alice felt gratitude to the men in her life who did not fall into the male stereotype. Men like Hastings and Stocking, who, seeing her talent and determination, helped clear the way for her forward and upward march.

Then everything changed and nothing changed. Alice, without having to take a step off the Wisconsin campus, accepted her first job. How it came about was uncommonly easy.

****

In her memoirs, Alice said, "Apparently realizing ... that I was better adapted to research than teaching, Prof. Hastings offered me the position of bacteriologist representing the dairy division on a team which was searching for methods to improve the flavor of cheddar cheese."

Alice accepted; her uneasiness ended. She became a Federal Civil Service Employee on July 1. But Wisconsin, not Washington, D.C., would be her workplace.

Why were Alice and her team of other bacteriologists not reporting for work at the Agriculture Department in Washington, D.C.?

It was a matter of overcrowding. The federal government was hiring scientific researchers as fast as they could recruit them. But the laboratory space needed for this growth did not yet exist. Construction workers were laboring long hours to finish an addition to the east wing of the white marble building called the Department of Agriculture.

In the meantime, state experimental stations, housed at various universities around the country, had agreed to collaborate with the federal government, which paid the salaries. Professors who directed operations and chose their own teams headed these stations.

Alice's career began with no fanfare. But oh! that splendid, steady paycheck! Besides, her boss was a friend and mentor. She had been in Madison long enough to have a social life. She had published four papers as a junior author with Prof. Hastings, as she worked toward her master's degree.

Alice tried heroically to remain motivated in the journey past the first few milestones of her career. She recorded that it was "...interesting, but not so stimulating as most of my later, more independent investigations."

Once, a photographer came to Alice's workspace; flashed an exposure of her as she concentrated at her wooden laboratory table. Decades later, Alice was to find a surprise in her mail, a package containing a photograph and a warm newsy letter from Prof. O.N. Allen. The professor had been Alice's teacher at Wisconsin, where he was still connected.

The picture was captioned, "Young Lady in Lab., Jan. 13, 1912." No prints had ever been made, Allen said, until he found the negative while sorting out old materials, He was, however, pretty sure of Alice's identity. He asked that she autograph the photo and return it to the college history department, promising to send her a personal copy. Alice replied:

"...When I opened the packet marked 'photograph' and recognized myself, I had to laugh, it was such a surprise to see a photograph of myself taken forty-four years ago which I do not remember having seen before. I could not think where you had obtained it until I read your letter. Then I recognized the work table and other features of the room, and my mind wandered over 'this young lady in lab' who was so hopeful in those days and eager to venture into research. If she could have foreseen the rough stretches in the road ahead, so well as the fulfillment of hopes, she could hardly have been so lighthearted..."

Lighthearted truly described Alice in her first job. Such peace. No more bedeviling financial worries! She now had money to enrich the quality of her life. She splurged by enrolling in a German language class – which added to her enjoyment of German culture as well as being useful in her career. Scientific Germany, in those years, led the world in bacteriology. Knowing the language meant that Alice could access German medical journals quickly.

One of her hopes was to further her studies in bacteriology at the University of Chicago. The university, then as now, was greatly esteemed for its high caliber of teaching and research. Alice wanted to meet some of the faculty in bacteriology and see for herself the laboratories. She would have to wait, however, to realize her dream.

WASHINGTON, D.C.

1913-1940

The new laboratory in Washington, D.C. awaited her and other Federal Civil Service researchers from around the country as they converged at the capitol city, leaving behind their campus lives. Exactly three years to the day since beginning her career at Wisconsin, Alice said good-by to midwestern friends and teachers. She flittered inwardly, her feelings mixed. How wondrous to be poised on the rim toward a flight into a fresh, unknown world. How scary to wonder about what she would find upon landing!

Ever practical, she planned a train stop in Chicago to visit the University of Chicago. Who knows what good could come out of exploring one's dream in advance?

Dr. Norman Harris, an assistant professor, met Alice in his office there. He led her through the university's bacteriology laboratories and classrooms. They sat, afterwards, and got acquainted.

"Where are you now employed?" he asked.

"I'm on my way to Washington," Alice said. "I have a position in the Dairy Division of the Bureau of Animal Industry."

Prof. Harris snapped to attention.

"Well! I am surprised to hear you say that, for I was there only a few weeks ago," he said, "and I was told that they did not want any women scientists."

Alice, startled at the professor's frankness, tried to keep her emotions from showing. This was not at all the picture Prof. Hastings had painted. Alice smoothed absentmindedly and without success, at the wrinkles in the lap of her long, navy blue dress. Then she rose and took a polite leave.

Later she wrote, "That night, speeding along on the train, the absurdity of my situation did not seem funny. I was on my way to Washington, where I had not wanted to go, and where I was not wanted. I arrived on...one of the summer's hottest days."

She could have said "one of the capitol city's hottest days", for Madison, Wisconsin, had few tropical, humid days. Nor did her hometown in Pennsylvania. Alice closed her eyes in the sweltering railroad car and pictured in her mind the cool, grassy banks of the creek, saw the wary grouse feeding close by, almost smelled the wildflowers and hayfields.

The city still sizzled on the day when Alice found, reporting for work at the Department of Agriculture, "a number of women scientists." Actually, the percentage of men to women was greatly skewed, but Alice was surprised to see any females at all. Some of the women had transferred from the Bureau of Chemistry; a few still worked there. Their jobs were with a department run by the Pure Food and Drug Act, a federal law passed in 1906. Several of the luckier female scientists were associates of Dr. Erwin Smith. He became famous for his pioneer efforts in finding career openings for women in his specialty of plant pathology.

"Most of his associates in the laboratory," Alice said, "were young women whom he had trained."

It was a different story in the Bureau of Animal Industry, a division of the Agriculture Department. Alice discovered she was the second female scientist in the bureau's history. She never found out the fate of the first woman. "...She left before I came," Alice remembered, always to wonder how this first woman "...happened to be admitted."

Alice knew how she, herself, happened to be admitted. She reasoned that the officers at the Bureau of Animal Industries unwittingly "...had left a loophole in the barrier [against women]." Innocently, Alice had squeezed through it!

She went on to explain. "When the arrangement was made for the professor in charge to select a civil service employee, [as was the case with Alice and Dr. Stocking] the thought had not occurred to them that a woman might be chosen."

All involved knew that Alice represented a new and challenging problem. By law, a civil service employee can be fired only because of a serious complaint. Alice was bound to hear rumors, those first days in Washington, about reactions of the bureau big-wigs. We can almost see Alice hunching her shoulders, dark eyes laughing, as she quoted a stenographer.

"When the bad news broke," Alice wrote, "...that a woman would be coming to join the staff...they nearly fell off their chairs."

The good news was that Alice did not have to spend eight hours a day with the administrators. Surprisingly, she found the dairy division a decent place to be. Her chiefs, Dr. B.H. Rawl and Dr. Lore Rogers, in charge of research, accepted her completely.

They explained the current investigations. One was to check on methods of manufacturing butter and cheese; another involved raw milk and pasteurization.

Pasteurization of liquids in these early days, called the Batch Method, consisted of heating the product to a temperature of 143 degrees Fahrenheit for 30 minutes, then chilling it quickly to 50 degrees Fahrenheit or less. Today the Continuous Process method of pasteurization is faster. Milk is heated to 161 degrees F. for 15 seconds, cooled quickly to 50 degrees F or below, and of course, kept cool until it is used.

(Alice had not a wisp of an idea what this new work had in store for her. But she would spawn a controversy that caused shock waves through the lands of commercial dairy producers all over the United States.)

Lastly, Alice's supervisors told her, she would apply herself to all other dairy problems that might be solved using basic sciences.

****

The noted science-writer, Paul de Kruif, described her

as being "…a pleasant-looking dark-eyed and retiring girl bacteriologist, buried away among other anonymous girl and boy bacteriologists…" Alice was 29 years old!

She continued her job as a junior collaborator in the same investigations she had pursued at the University of Wisconsin. But these studies she said, "did not occupy my full time." She was gratified and excited, when the opportunity came for her to take a course in mycology at the University of Chicago. Her dream of studying at this famous school was coming true, but she never imagined that the course would be botany, one dealing with fungi.

Before she left for Illinois, a decision by Dr. Charles Thom to leave the dairy division, would point Alice toward her destiny. Dr. Thom had been studying the effect of fungi, particularly the <u>Penicillium</u> genus on cheese flavor. He resigned from the department the next year, 1914, but stayed in other branches of the Department of Agriculture until he retired. During that time he grew to be an authority in mycology. History now recognizes his remarkable contribution to health (animal and human) which came from his pioneering method to mass-produce penicillin.

Dr. Thom's departure meant changes within the department. It fell to Alice to take on the task of "keeping the cultures pure and providing subcultures for the experiments." The experiments could be called commercial, for they were intended to find better ways of manufacturing cheese flavors.

Alice took the advice of her chief and spent one term at the University of Chicago.

Reading between the lines in her memoirs, it appears her vision of doing intriguing graduate work at the famous university dissolved while she was in Chicago. Dryly humorous, she said later, "My memory is dim about how much use I made of my newly-acquired knowledge of mycology but I remember it did not interfere greatly with the progress in a research problem in which I was much interested."

This "research problem," along with Alice's shift in laboratory duties, would turn out to be her gateway to fame.

Chapter 6

The Breakthrough

*"I wanted to know more about
these organisms."*
— Alice Evans

In the months before Alice went to Chicago, she had been allowed to labor on "a problem that was my very own." More and more she felt herself drawn to the phenomenon of bacteria in freshly-drawn milk. What happened in the cow's udder, microbe-wise? How important were the bacteria excreted in that milk? A host of questions followed her to the University of Chicago. That fall quarter of 1914, instead of her course work taking first place in her time and interest, Alice found herself planning experiments with sample milk cultures that she managed to get from cows supplying the area with milk. Specifically, they were taken from the animal under germ-free conditions to prevent any outside contamination.

Alice felt like she had won the Irish Sweepstakes!

These obscure bacteria began to overtake her thoughts. The single mycology course she relegated to a tiny portion of her brain. Some nights sleep couldn't come for having to compete with Alice's mental experiments with the priceless milk samples. She could hardly wait to get back to Washington.

Generous, far-sighted Dr. Rogers, her chief, "had wisely given only general directions to research workers, leaving them free to follow the leads that their own observations detected." Alice plunged into researching cow's bacterial flora.

Around her shone a dazzling light of collegial acceptance and assistance. At this lustrous time, Alice felt no discrimination; her co-workers were supportive and helpful. She had only to request materials and they were quickly and cheerfully granted.

"My attention," she said, "was gradually focused on one particular species, ...[Bacillus abortus or B. abortus]" This is the organism which causes animals to lose their young by miscarriage. This microbe along with Micrococcus melitensis or M. Melitensis would be renamed in 1920 in honor of its discoverer, Dr. David Bruce.

Painstakingly reading reports from 1910-12 studies, Alice knew that B. abortus not only existed in infected cows, but also in seemingly healthy animals. Dr. Theobald Smith (who was later to be a powerful critic of Alice's future discovery) and an associate reported this finding. A similar study by Schroeder and Cotton of the Bureau of Animal Industries found B. abortus in cow's milk and both reports warned that these bacteria might be dangerous to humans. "The idea of drinking milk contaminated with bacteria capable of causing disease in animals was distasteful

48

to me," Alice said. "I wanted to know more about these organisms. Especially, I wanted to know whether they were related to any species known to cause human disease."

Alice deliberated and dug into the nature of B. abortus. She needed clues that might link this bacteria to other harmful bacteria. Dr. Eichhorn, a chief in the division of pathology, was one of the first persons Alice consulted.

What a splendid move it turned out to be! When she asked Dr. Eichhorn, in a soft but clearly enunciated voice, if he knew of any healthy animal that had given off pathogenic (toxic) bacteria to humans, he nodded.

"Yes," he said, "Milk from apparently healthy goats can carry the germs of human undulant fever."

To Alice's carefully prepared questions, Dr. Eichhorn responded helpfully. He gave her "pertinent information", but, she said emphatically, the pathologist himself had never connected the goat (Micrococcus melitensis) and cow (Bacillus abortus) organisms as being related when they discussed the organisms. Later, during an interview, Alice recalled that Dr. Eichhorn had asked, almost casually, if she had thought of comparing the Bang bacillus (B. abortus) with the Bruce bacillus, (M. Melitensis). Alice had shaken her head.

Once settled in at her work-station she mulled over the words that had passed between them. If the doctor had considered a connection between the two microbes, he could not have figured it to be a reasonable one. Otherwise, why hadn't he himself gone forward with the study? She knew that Danish Dr. Bang, one of the princes of science, the finder of Bacillus abortus in 1896, had never mentioned the possibility of a bug brotherhood.

Eichhorn's remark did ignite an idea for Alice. When

she revealed her new project, however, colleagues smiled. Alice, they said fondly, was off and running. (Later, someone, not Dr. Eichhorn, suggested that it had been he who made the connection between the two microbes. Alice typically objective, but leaving no doubt, set the record straight in her autobiography.)

Alice sought a match, a likening between two microbes no scientist had reckoned as being similar. She knew that <u>M. melitensis</u>, the goat bacterium and <u>B. abortus</u>, the cow bacterium, infected udders of outwardly healthy animals. What more compelling reason could there be, she thought, than to look for other characteristics in common?

Keen with enthusiasm, Alice shrugged into a white lab coat each morning and attacked the new project. It's a frontier, Alice thought, and I don't have a clue to where it will lead. Her pulses throbbed as she prepared cultures, peered through her microscope, made notes. She was often only dimly aware of coworkers and activities surrounding her. Had noon hour really come and gone? How could it be time for end-of-day cleaning?

Plunging into comparative research of the two organisms, she sent away for sample bacteria.

Alice counted the hours until the specimens came from the American Museum of Natural History. One was a tube of "Malta fever" microbes (<u>M. melitensis</u>) Dr. David Bruce had taken from the body of an English serviceman 21 years before. The museum laboratory had kept these organisms alive by feeding them beef-broth jelly. The other five strains she got from the Bureau of Animal Industry. They were not identified as to whether they came from humans or goats. That they were vaguely labeled, "prior to 1900 - to 1909", added mystery, which she could have done without.

As the months passed, Alice's excitement escalated and her convictions grew firm. She studied the goat microbes under the microscope until her neck and shoulder muscles cramped. It seemed to Alice, finally, that it would be a miracle if they did not belong to the same family.

Paul de Kruif, with his usual flair, said this about Alice's new work: "By all that was strange, perverse, topsy-turvy... the bug of Bruce from sick and dead human beings, the bug of Bang from poor calves born too soon – did look alike!"

What Alice had done was to pull off all the labels from the cultures she received from the museum so she would not know which was which. She painted them with dye. Then she ran the test again and studied the results, her heartbeat quickening. Some should be different from the others, but they all looked alike!

Daily, those months in 1917, growing more fired-up each time she guardedly lifted the racks of distinctive germs from the incubators, Alice compared and compared again. She grew the microbes in agar-agar jelly, on potatoes, in milk. After a week's incubation, some turned a bit browner than others. Was that important?

Uncertain, knowing she needed more data, Alice went to the pathology department in the Bureau of Animal Industry. There, hesitating because dairy folks were not encouraged to use live animals, she asked Dr. John Buck if he could spare some pregnant guinea pigs.

"Of course, little lady!" the pathologist boomed. "What for?"

"Well," Alice said, greatly relieved but wondering how much she should tell this doctor, "I might be on to a relationship between the Bang and Bruce bacilli."

"Hmmm, interesting," the pathologist said, and Alice smiled to herself. If I'm right, she thought, a lot of suffering and death can be averted. If I'm wrong, I'm just another foolish female.

She handed the doctor a rack of small bottles. "I've prepared some serums," she said, in a small voice, "and I'll need eight animals."

Having planned the experiment precisely, Alice directed Dr. Buck to inject four of the guinea pigs with a culture taken from humans infected with B. abortus. Another four received a strain of B. abortus she recently had obtained from a cow's fetus.

Her mouth dry from nervousness, Alice returned to her work-station and tried not to think about what might be happening in the guinea pig cages. She didn't have long to agonize. In a few days, three animals in each group aborted. Five days after inoculation, Alice ordered one animal killed from each group. She cultivated, by agar slope culture, B. abortus from the organs of both animals. Eight days later another animal in each group was killed. From their organs, Alice again made agar slope cultures. Within three to four days the characteristic dewdrop colonies made their appearance on both set of slopes. "No distinction," Alice told an interviewer later, "could be found between the growths of the organism until the slopes had been incubated for several weeks..."

And in her laboratory, as Alice scrutinized these cultures, holding within herself a desperate wish to find affirmation of her peculiar theory, she saw in this final stage only one difference – the old human culture from Malta eventually turned more brown than the others. Seventeen years later,

Dr. I. Forest Huddleson answered this nagging question in his book about brucella infections. (The microbes would be classified after 1920 as a species of the genus, Brucella.) He determined that browning on growth of most <u>Br. melitensis</u> and a few of the <u>Br. abortus</u> on agar and potato slants is normal.

Reflecting on what she had found in these silent, tiny creatures, Alice let the intoxication of the discovery warm her blood. With a rush of energy she tidied up her workplace. Her feet ran unnecessary errands instead of breaking into a dance.

Yet Alice, searching for truth, needed more proof. Had she dug out even a portion of the truth? For twenty years bacteriologists classified these microbes into different families. What if her own studies turned out to be a fluke - a terrible coincidence - or worse yet, the product of faulty experimentation?

She perched on the wooden laboratory stool and wrote in careful penmanship details of the guinea pig experiment. So much to do! Long after other workers went home, Alice stayed on. If hunger and fatigue visited, she paid no attention. There was one more acceptable test, a final, decisive study, using blood. One, that if she did not do, would haunt her forever.

Alice prepared a salt-water solution. Slowly she added the fluid to hundreds of thousands of human Malta fever bacteria which waited in tiny glass bottles. She saw the solution whirl, change to a milky color.

Turning to another rack of small tubes, she repeated the activity. These tubes, however, held great numbers of cow abortion bacteria. This fluid also took on a cloudy appearance.

Lastly, she dripped, into all the tubes, equal amounts of a cow's diluted blood serum. This particular cow had been given shots containing B. abortus making it immune – it would never get sick with the Bang microbe. Alice knew this immune animal's blood, when tested, should clump together in a salt solution with only the B. abortus microbes and no others.

She placed the racks in an incubator; turned away to attend to other matters. The experiment would not be ready to remove until long after the building emptied of workers.

Minutes and hours had never crept so slowly. At last, her breath quickening, Alice bent and tenderly removed the racks; set them on the workbench. Now she would know with certainty. No chance for errors here. The cells would clump together or they would not. Adjusting her small, round pincer-type glasses more securely on her nose, she witnessed the realization of her prayers.

The salt water in all the tubes had cleared!

Alice pulled up a lab stool and lowered herself to it, dazed by the spectacle. Even the tube contents into which she had dripped a tiny amount of blood serum had transformed! Her dark eyes, now glowing, were riveted to the bottom of the tubes. There lay the telltale clumps of white sediment! It was over. The two microbes were not only related, they were twins!

Chapter 7

Discovery!

*"Discoveries have
reverberations..."*
– Patricia McLaughlin

Twelve years later, Alice said to an interviewer, "I am sure that sight was the greatest thrill of my life. I was all alone there...everybody else had gone home...alone with those racks of tubes."

In December of 1917, four years after entering the new marble building, Alice went before the meeting of the Society of American Bacteriologists, held in Washington, D.C., a diminutive figure, standing on the podium before an audience of which few were women. Alice read her paper. It was entitled, "The Large Numbers of Bact. Abortus... Which May Be Found In Milk."

Summing up the results of her investigations, Alice said, "Considering the close relationship between the two organisms, and the reported frequency of virulent (disease-laden) strains of <u>B. abortus</u> in cow's milk, it would seem remarkable that we do not have a disease resembling Malta fever in this country." She went on to pose a question.

"Are we sure that the cases of glandular disease, or cases of abortion, or possibly disease of the respiratory tract may not sometimes occur among human subjects in this country as a result of drinking raw cow's milk?"

Alice's worst apprehensions did not come close to the powerful reaction which followed. The men in the conference challenged her immediately in the question-and-answer period, stumbling over each other's words to query her. "If these organisms are closely related, why has not some other scientist noted it?" they bristled.

Alice wished she could say, bluntly, what would be received as blasphemy. She wanted to say, "No one else has found this truth, because in the poverty of your imagination it is easier to believe that the printed word is gospel truth. I went beyond the realms of your perceptions."

Instead she replied, "Your criticism is not valid. A few hours work of any bacteriologist who has the (proper) cultures at hand, could test the accuracy of my report."

But they would not accept her cool common-sense approach. One way or another, the men, by innuendo or in outright hostility, let her know how they felt about a woman, one without a medical doctor's degree, having the gall to take up their time with such silliness. Some physicians then and in the decade following turned their backs to her at meetings.

The timing of Alice's discovery could not have been worse. Tuberculosis in cows had become epidemic, and the dairy industry reeled from the loss. Beautiful, healthy-looking cows had to be slaughtered if they tested positive to the T.B. germ. With a passion, dairymen rejected this woman who tried to convince them that their cows might be responsible for another human disease. Besides, they thundered, pasteurization was costly and uncalled for. All dairymen knew, they said, that the Commission of Milk Standards, made up from professions in public health, sanitation, bacteriology, medicine, etc., in various locations in the United States advised that market milk should be clearly labeled with a grade A, B, or C.

Alice explained in her Memoirs, Chapter VII, "Milk as a Carrier of Disease" about milk grading and certification. "Grade A milk might be either raw or pasteurized," she wrote. "Grade A raw milk should be drawn and bottled under strict conditions of cleanliness; it should be from cows free from disease as determined by tuberculin testing and by physical examinations made by qualified veterinarians; it should be handled by employees free from disease as determined by a qualified physician, under sanitary conditions such that the bacterial count should not exceed 10,000 per cubic centimeter. [This raw milk was the certified milk so highly regarded by dairymen.]

"The qualifications for Grade A pasteurized milk," she continued, "were somewhat lower. Grades B and C were of inferior quality but were required to meet the standards for those grades."

The Commission on Milk Standards had recommended pasteurization of milk in reports it published in 1912 and 1913. But since the bacterial content was the prime factor in grading milk the commission excluded certified milk from the pasteurization advisory believing that medical inspections and adherence to cleanliness rules would be a guarantee against infectious germs of communicable diseases. The commission, therefore, did not take seriously the U.S. Public Health service report stating its belief that pasteurization of milk is the only effective means of eliminating communicable disease germs.

Alice felt no surprise at being rebuffed for blaming yet another infectious disease on cow's milk. Doctors largely misdiagnosed "Malta fever", believing that it did not exist in this country. Why then, should she expect bacteriologists and other medical scientists to accept her theory without reservations?

Alice found that in the brotherhood of medical research and business her discovery was being criticized as often as it was ignored. There were, however, a few researchers who read her history avidly. One of them was Swiss-born Dr. Karl Meyer and his colleague, Simin Fleischner. Dr. Meyer had emigrated to San Francisco California, where he and his partner also studied <u>B. abortus</u>. Meyer, a huge man, with handsome, deep-set eyes, a rough mustache, and a hobby of mountain climbing, would prove to be a long-distance colleague to Alice.

Now, a bit more than a year has passed since Alice's painful revelation. She has turned to other research. But at home, in a comfortable reading chair with its floor lamp, Alice not only kept up-to-date with current scientific journals, she researched what had been done in pioneer studies. One evening Alice was leafing through a new journal when the words "Malta fever" and "Mediterranean fever" jumped out at her. Turning quickly back to the title page she noted that the author was Dr. Meyer. With great interest and satisfaction, Alice learned that he had tested seemingly healthy milk cows in the San Francisco area. Each testing of these "certified" milk cows had shown the microbe <u>B. abortus</u> to be present.

It was Meyer and his collaborators, some two years later, who came up with the suggestion that an additional bacterial genus be recognized -<u>Brucella</u>- which would include the bacteria then called <u>Micrococcus melitensis</u> and <u>Bacillus abortus</u>. It was quickly adopted.

"But aside from that [Meyer's report] almost nobody would believe me," Alice said later to an interviewer. "That wasn't surprising, because the whole business of these supposedly different microbes being identical twins, was too simple. If that were true, somebody else would have run on to it long before." Alice smiled at the reporter. Her small, dainty features lit up. It was plain she held no bitterness.

Back at the laboratory, she had not let the opposition upset her. Dr. Rogers paved the way and seven months later, (July, 1918) the report she had read at the Society of Bacteriologists was published in the Journal of Infectious Diseases. Alice heard more rumblings.

If the American scientists were not suspicious of this nondescript woman, they were skeptical. Alice explained in detail later.

"There was a reason," she wrote, "why bacteriologists had never noticed a resemblance between the two sources. The early British investigators considered the causal organism of Malta fever to be spherical, and they placed it in the genus <u>Micrococcus</u> with other spherical species."

She went on, saying that Dr. Bernhard Bang, a Danish veterinarian, and recognized finder of the organism which causes abortion in cows, considered it to be rod-shaped. Thus he placed it in a group with other rod-shaped species.

Alice, ever careful and cautious, established that some

of the Malta fever organisms were indeed, rod-shaped. But they often divided, she said, in such a way that they were shortened, and appeared under a microscope, to be round or spherical.

Thus, because no bacteriologist would ever think of relating the two species because of their shape, the discovery had gone by the way until Alice's work with pregnant guinea pigs.

An intriguing story came to light when Alice mentioned that, as far as she could determine, the only other man who had come to the same conclusion as she about human Malta fever was a German. (In her memoirs, she did not identify this man.) World War I, he claimed, kept his research out of publication. In the United States, years later, A.J. Cronin wrote the novel, Shannon's Way. In it, the fictitious leading character labored hard and long to come up with the same results as had Alice and the German scientist. Cronin's plot has the character on the verge of publishing his findings. A friend enters the critical scene, telling him the crushing news that an American woman had just published "his" facts! It is more than possible the novelist read newspaper accounts of Alice's retirement in 1945, which mentioned Alice's accomplishments, for Shannon's Way came out in 1948.

True, she was yet an unknown scientist. In 1922, when Alice talked about her discovery to a reporter, she had no medical degree or even a doctor of philosophy degree.

When asked if she were aware of the world-wide human implications of her discovery, Alice replied in her usual understatement.

"Sort of vaguely I knew what it meant," she said. "I knew most American milk wasn't pasteurized. I'd just proved there was no practical difference between the abortion germ and the Malta fever [germ]."

She knew for certain she would be shunned or met with hostility by those whose livelihood or professional status she had challenged. Gracefully, sometimes humorously, Alice met the attackers. Her character matured; her remarkable intellect, her shy persistence in the search for the truth, and always, her interest in and care for others carried her forward. Alice, child of a proud family who never reached material success, grew up rich in cultural advantage, quietly poised, a woman of class.

Chapter 8

Music and Friendships

*"Friendship of a kind that cannot
easily be reversed tomorrow must
have its roots in common interests
and shared beliefs..."*
– Barbara Tuchman

To succeed, Alice knew she must provide balance in
her life. A whole, loving personality did not come out of
someone who let herself become work-obsessed. Music,
an integral part of her Welsh upbringing, provided this
balance during the years she sang as a choir member. Her
church was the Mt. Pleasant (now Westmoreland)
Congregational Church in Washington, D.C.

On choir practice night, Alice usually prepared herself
a simple meal, and after eating, cleaned the kitchen. She
hated clutter and disorganization; coming home late and
tired to face dirty dishes and pots was unthinkable.

Alice, because she was short, found herself being a

leader of the processional line that took her to a "conspicuous" corner seat in the choir loft each Sunday morning!

That noticeable location, during an evening performance of Gounod's "St. Cecilia's Mass" three years later, made for a heady experience.

In the audience that night, was the director of the Department of Agriculture chorus.

"Apparently, he recognized me as the lone woman scientist of the Bureau of Animal Industry," Alice said.

One day, the director, Mr. Roberts, went to the laboratory where Alice was working with her cultures.

After introducing himself, he came directly to the point.

"I'm looking for additional chorus members," he said. "There's a special event coming up. President [Woodrow] Wilson is going to deliver a Flag Day Address. Several government departments" he went on, "are now rehearsing selections to sing for the occasion."

Alice's first thought was to decline. Mr. Roberts saw the hesitation on her face.

"I want you to sit in the front row of seats behind the President," he added.

Alice held up her hands and laughed.

"Mr. Roberts, you obviously think that all us Welsh have outstanding voices. I assure you, that is not the case with me! My voice is not strong enough to justify my occupying so prominent a seat."

The chorus director could not be dissuaded. Finally, thinking to herself that he probably believed she was a great singer wanting to be coaxed, she agreed to join.

So it happened, that warm day in June, 1916, Alice sat,

"a few feet from President Wilson, with no one between us." She looked out upon a large noonday mass of people. Many of them were government workers, who had either given up their lunch hour or had brought sandwiches with them. She listened, a little self-conscious of her conspicuous placement, as the President spoke. His speech was entitled, This Nation Is Again To Be Tested.

Roberts' belief in the musical superiority of the Welsh was a common conception then, and certainly well deserved. Welsh talents in music flowered in the Protestant churches they formed, and congregations of ordinary people sang hymns in four-part harmony. So honored were they by others musically inclined, that non-Welsh churches sometimes lured them away to be choir directors, soloists and choir members. Many children of immigrants grew up to be entertainers and music teachers.

In the coal mines, both in Wales and the eastern United States, laborers sang as they worked; heavenly music relieved their drudgery in the black, hellish depths. One of their most loved composers was William Aubrey Williams, who called himself Gwilym Gwent. During his life as a miner, he composed anthems, popular songs for glee clubs, cantatas and hymns. In 1871, he sailed to the United States, and lived his last 20 years as a Pennsylvania miner and conductor of choirs and brass bands. Often, inspiration hit while he worked. When this happened, he whipped out a stub of chalk from his pocket and quickly scrawled the musical notes on the side of a coal car. At quitting time, he transferred his creation to a scrap of paper to take home and finish. His countrymen called him "Mozart of the Coal Fields."

The custom of eisteddfod, a Welsh poetry and musical

celebration, came to America in 1850. It encouraged creative expression in spectacular festivals both local and national, each year. There were superbly rehearsed vocal soloists, trios, glee clubs, and the largest choirs that could be gathered – some groups were 300 strong. Mendelssohn, Handel and Hayden were favorite grand choral composers, and the competition was fierce for first place (prize: $1,000). The glees liked to perform temperance ditties such as "Avoid the Cup" and one local eisteddfod drew an entry from a 10-year-old boy singing, "Have Courage, My Boy, To Say No."

For two weeks in the summer of 1921 Alice vacationed at Chautauqua, New York. She joined a large chorus to sing Handel's <u>Messiah</u>, a composition she had most likely memorized in her many years of performing religious music. As a finale to this "glorious performance the chorus and distinguished soloists were accompanied by the New York Philharmonic Orchestra." At this peak, Alice left her hobby, realizing that her life needed to be sorted out. She wrote, "The highest point of my choral activities was reached at their ending."

But why would Alice leave her cherished hobby? What needed to be reorganized within her life? If we flash forward in time, we will see that Alice contracts undulant fever after World War I has ended. It is likely, although she did not specify the reasons in the memoirs, that this first terrifying bout of the disease left her weak and hurting. Certainly good reason to cease activities not absolutely connected to survival.

Let us return to late 1917. For years Alice had signed in as the only female scientist in the Dairy Division. When World War I torpedoed its way to the United States it gloomed even the most optimistic. Alice would find her work agenda changed. Brother Morgan was not called to serve in the armed forces. He had married Zoe Dyer in Ohio and had a baby daughter, Anna. As a plant breeder, his work was important to the war effort.

The terrible disease, epidemic meningitis, was one of several infections which weakened our country's armed services. A victim of meningitis often had less than a 50% chance of surviving. Alice saw that her skills were needed immediately in this research area. Sensibly, she set aside the Malta fever research, sighing inwardly at hard choices and inquired at the Hygienic Laboratory about research possibilities.

Alice learned that a position was open for a bacteriologist. She had not made the decision lightly; indeed, in Alice's well-ordered life she gave every resolution careful thought. The Dairy Division was no place to move ahead in the study of Malta fever; the Hygienic Laboratory held the keys to whatever career doors needed to be opened. She would, of course, devote her skills whole-heartedly to the war effort. With the return of peace, back to melitensis and abortus research!

Fondly, she recalled Dr. Rawls, chief of her division, saying good-by and how he had stressed his willingness to welcome her back to the Dairy division should the move prove unsatisfactory. Alice felt great affection for her colleagues there. She devoted three long paragraphs in Memoirs telling of her appreciation and total support from co-workers. No restraints hampered her, she said. They supplied cheerfully all her needs, even providing animals for research along with the willing help of pathologists, whom, she said, frankly expressed skepticism. Dr. Rogers,

66

ever loyal, had smoothed her path to publication in medical journals.

She was touched by Rawls' sincere offer, but wrote later, "I never requested the return transfer because my interest expanded…" The interest, naturally, being her dream of exposing bacteria-contaminated milk and milk products which she now was sure caused the insidious disease, Malta fever.

With the transfer, Alice stepped into another world. A varied world with different goals, where a hundred souls toiled, all strangers to her this April day in 1918.

That fateful spring morning Alice walked toward the red brick building on 25th and E Street, N.W. She ascended the hill and turned to look down at the wide, historic Potomac River.

When the days grew tropically hot, she would know why the natives called the area "Foggy Bottom." She would see the steam rise from the Potomac and combine with vapors given off by a nearby brewery and a gas works. With the putrid smell of garbage-strewn slum housing, the combination resulted in a dismal gray haze; such was the summer setting of the Hygienic Laboratory.

The service she was about to enter actually began in 1798 as the Marine Hospital Service on Staten Island in New York. The laboratory started out in one room with Dr. Joseph Kinyoun as its only full-time staff member. He was charged with using his newly acquired skills in bacteriology to screen arriving European passengers for cholera as well as gearing up to fight epidemic disease. The laboratory was renamed Public Health and Marine Hospital Service after a move to Washington, D.C.

In 1912, when Alice was working for the Dairy Division,

the laboratory service became simply, the Public Health Service. In earlier days the laboratory's duty had been to investigate "infectious and contagious diseases and matters of public health". Scientists here helped with investigations and control of certain epidemic diseases. They also tested and regulated vaccines and other biologic products. With new legislation the laboratory's mission grew to include studying non-infectious diseases and water-pollution.

But now, what and who awaited inside the brick walls behind her? Alice knew from making inquiries that she would be the only researcher not holding a doctor's degree. Where would that put her in the pecking order? Would her strong positive experiences of the past years perhaps cause her to expect too much?

She turned and pulled open the dark, heavy doors, her heart rattling against her chest, and was greeted by Dr. McCoy. Sweet-tempered, self-effacing George McCoy, destined to become the most influential person in her life since childhood, escorted her up the stairs to the second floor, east end, to her work-station. Along the way smiling faces acknowledged Alice's entry into the new family.

Quickly, warmly, she became a member of a team of medical doctors in the Division of Pathology and Bacteriology, who were "trying to improve the antiserum used in the treatment of epidemic meningitis." This type of infection is commonly called spinal meningitis and the disease goes straight to the brain from the nose and throat, with no infection developing there first. A fast-acting terrifying disease.

The equipment was simple, but as good, Alice thought, as in any other government laboratory. The team had to be thrifty, for war expenses made a massive drain on the treasury.

The war years, grim and shocking as they were, brought a sardonic twist regarding women's struggle for careers. The armed forces had drafted nearly all of our country's budding scientists and left universities as well as the Hygienic Laboratory nearly bereft of men. But research and epidemic control, now more than ever, had to be continued and accelerated. Truly desperate, the medical chiefs turned to the few previously unnoticed women toiling in the depths of the laboratories. Administrators assigned them the work of the men at less pay, and aggressively began to encourage schools to train women in science. Everywhere laboratories reached out to women. The doors to the sacred rooms flew open and the password changed from "I am a man" to "I am a scientist." And of course, women trained and entered.

Alice would work there for 19 years under Chief George McCoy, a time she described as a "brilliant period of the institution." Dr. McCoy, she said, topped the list of distinguished scientists. He wore his hair combed high off his forehead, a pompadour, it was called, and his eyes, intelligent, penetrating but friendly, looked down at little Alice with ease and warmth. A tall man, thin, rugged, McCoy had earned fame for his labors on leprosy, a contagious disease caused by a bacillus. He also directed for 13 years the U.S. Plague Laboratory in San Francisco which discovered that ground squirrels could cause tularemia (Rabbit fever) in humans. At the Hygienic Laboratory, he researched problems in other diseases, in addition to administering the institute.

Alice would come to realize that McCoy, as director of the department's finances, had been given a tight budget by the government. With a master hand, he hired talented women scientists who had to accept much lower wages than men doing the same work. In addition, women seldom received job advancements in title or salary. The personally generous McCoy will always be remembered for his inspired efforts to encourage women workers toward excellence and for using employment practices far ahead of his time. With reason, in the late 1920's, a Hygienic Laboratory biochemist, Helen Dyer, grumbled that McCoy refused to give single women raises in salary. (Possibly a more accurate analysis would be to say that McCoy did not promote women to levels of greater responsibility.) Several laboratory workers were women. Had they been married, they would not have been considered for the work! Yet, we will see why Alice wrote, "He gave luster to the laboratory."

A colorful secret came to light in the form of an entry from the Hygienic Laboratory log thought to be in the late 1920's. Dr. McCoy had secretly met two leprosy sufferers at a boat in Norfolk, Virginia. The outcasts were enroute to the National Leprosarium in Carville, Louisiana. McCoy himself transported them by automobile to the Hygienic Laboratory. There he arranged for their comfort and had meals sent in from the Naval Hospital next door until it was time for the ship to depart for Louisiana.

He had labored long in leprosy research in Hawaii. During this time he classified almost 700 rat tumors from examination of some 100,000 rats, experience which made him stoutly believe that large-scale field investigations should march side-by-side with laboratory work in conquering epidemics and crippling diseases.

Alice also was fond of old Dr. Charles Stiles, and his mild eccentricities. Dr. Stiles had accomplished a major

70

achievement when his work freed rural United States from hookworm disease.

Sometimes the good doctor's oddness "added a little spice to life within the old brick building," Alice said. "One morning I was walking down New Hampshire to the laboratory, and had to wait, as usual, for a chance to pass the heavy eastbound traffic, for this was before the time of traffic lights on Pennsylvania Avenue. As I stood there, Dr. Stiles caught up with me and together we waited. He was wearing his khaki uniform, as was his custom, although other medical officers wore their uniforms only when necessary; and he was carrying a walking stick. Becoming impatient with the wait, he stepped into the street and held up his cane, signaling traffic to stop. It stopped and we proceeded."

A favorite of the staff was Dr. James Leake, a boyishly vigorous young man who never walked upstairs. He always ran taking two steps at a time. He had been in charge of serums and vaccines since 1913 at the laboratory and while working with Dr. John Force he originated the multiple pressure methods of vaccination. Leake was an expert in the contagions of smallpox, typhoid fever, tetanus and cerebrospinal meningitis. He was renowned for his studies of poliomyelitis (polio). At this time in medical history, scientists did not know the cause of poliomyelitis. Later, they would discover an infinitely tiny virus, not a bacterium, to be the etiological agent. Whenever there was an outbreak of disease in the country, he would pack a bag and be gone as long as it took to control.

Added to that, Alice said, was Leake's wonderfully "unifying, humanizing influence" on those around him. From the day she reported for work there, shaking inwardly, Dr. Leake made her feel comfortable, like a close family member. She never turned down an invitation to join the Leakes when they entertained in their gracious home. And always, Dr. Leake "was alert to see if he could be of service to any of us when help was needed."

In her retirement, when she reflected on the accomplishments of scientists in the Hygienic Laboratory, Alice realized that the years she devoted to this little kingdom, were surely priceless, golden times.

Alice, this first year, 1918, worked in the same building with two other women, both of whom, "were well established there." (She did hear about Mathilde L. Koch, niece of the great Dr. Koch. Miss Koch was a pharmacologist but no longer an employee, or even listed as a member of the laboratory group. She published in the laboratory bulletin, however, as a senior author in collaboration with a male doctor, whose name has been lost).

A woman definitely listed in the "laboratory corps" as its first female member was Ida A. Bengtson. She had been there about two years when Alice arrived. Outwardly, Ida appeared to be the most average of average; slight in stature, her brownish hair pulled back tightly and wound in a bun. Unassuming in demeanor, she could walk unprepared into a research problem, quietly take over and get to the heart of difficulty – fast!

At the time, Miss Bengtson was taking courses at the University of Chicago to complete a doctor's degree in bacteriology which she earned the next year. Alice saw in her a perfect personality as well as a superb scientist. Ida, Alice said, was a flexible, high-performance type; a tireless worker. Herself a quiet, gentle person, Alice used these exact words to describe her new friend and mentor.

Ida enjoyed thorough acceptance in a workplace where few men had her educational and personal attributes. Even in her early years at the laboratory, she wrote many articles on bacteriology as sole or senior author. Sometimes Ida collaborated with Chief McCoy and signed as junior author on published papers.

One of Ida's fine talents, Alice said, was teaching. Ida instructed incoming medical officers each year during orientation weeks.

Before she retired to her picturesque farm in the Blue Ridge Mountains, Ida Bengtson identified a new variety, "C", of an organism, whose toxin caused paralytic disease in chickens. Later, using the complement fixation test, she adapted it for finding and differentiating rickettsial (typhus) infections. Her labors in this field of tissue culture, leaning long hours over globes, test tubes, microscopes and chick embryos, helped lead the way to production of a vaccine against typhus rickettsial. This was a miracle for armed forces members and civilians alike during World War II, for this feared contagious organism sometimes killed more servicemen and women than combat. From 1934 to 1939 she "carried on basic studies which led to the establishment of official United States and international units for standardizing the antitoxins most commonly involved in cases of gas gangrene..." These words are from the obituary Alice wrote, which appeared in the Journal of the Washington Academy of Science in 1953.

Ida and Alice had a close, sisterly relationship which continued beyond their retirements in 1945. Both women were born in January of 1881. Sadly, Ida lived only seven years after leaving The National Institutes of Health. Heavy with sorrow, Alice sat down to write a detailed description of her friend's accomplishments.

A woman whose name was not written on the register at the Hygienic Laboratory, was Rose (Polly) Parrott. She hired in to support a study which was comparing raw and pasteurized milk. Cow's milk as a food for infants was a new idea. The knowledge that Alice would bring to light about the dangers of drinking raw milk proved to be very significant.

Everybody loved bouncy, merry Polly. Because of her skills she remained after completion of the study. Her title became "Expert Technician" and she assisted in all kinds of investigations.

But, tragically, "...One day in 1944 she became accidentally infected with a tularemia culture and died within a few days," Alice reported of her colleague.

Her coworkers were traumatized, although they faced daily the danger that took Polly's life. Alice, in 1965, wrote "...She was so much a part of the life of the institution, that she should have a place in (my) memoirs."

The laboratory became a second home to Alice, the equipment was her furniture, the doctors and other scientists, her family. The laboratory entertained an unique burnt smell caused by researchers sterilizing tools with bunsen burners, and singeing the cotton they used to wipe carbon from the instruments. The scuffed woodwork and peeling paint gave the big rooms a well-used look. Sometimes a lost mouse skittered to safety beneath a cabinet. Yet quiet victories triumphed here; months and years of plodding, tedious labor would suddenly burst into fruition and a terrible disease would be conquered. Alice thrived in the environment and if she had thoughts of marrying sometime and producing her own family, when it meant giving up an exciting and hard-won career, well, it was a lifestyle she never sought. Alice realized that society disapproved of a woman who tried to combine homemaking with a job. Few women Alice knew or heard about had managed to accomplish this, and those who did appeared to have husbands who strongly supported their efforts. Usually the contributions of married women were downgraded or ignored in the workplace.

Alice remained the spinster, the loving daughter, the maiden aunt. To her colleagues she was little Alice, brilliant, rock-steady, and loyal to a fault. When they teased her. asking, "How's our Pennsylvania hillbilly this morning?" she was quick to grin and fire back a witty answer. Nonetheless, Alice met with a frown remarks made in fun about her Welsh ancestry. She had the typical Welsh pride in her heritage.

A Public Health Service doctor-researcher who attained hero status within the Hygienic Laboratory for his vigorous dedication to the prevention and cure of human illness was Joseph Goldberger. When Alice worked in the Washington D.C. Dairy Division, she had heard intriguing tales about Dr. Goldberger who was researching the widespread disease of pellagra among the poor folks of the United States. A child of peasant tenant farmers from Czechoslovakia, he had settled with his family in New York City, studied medicine and hired in at the Marine Hospital Service in 1899, the parent agency of the Hygienic Laboratory.

Goldberger preferred the excitement of working at the scenes of epidemics. His presence usually meant that the area was danger-enshrouded, as in the typhus and yellow fever outbreaks, two greatly-feared sicknesses. Into the midst of misery and death he waded, not to emerge until he had reached a place in his research studies where he could go forward no more. His creative, dynamic style added to the knowledge of influenza, Rocky Mountain spotted fever, diphtheria and measles.

In 1914 Goldberger headed for the South with orders from the Hygienic Laboratory to discover what pellagra really was and to find a cure. The assignment appealed to his fighting spirit and he quickly immersed himself in research of the disease which included a sore mouth, and the three "D's" - diarrhea, dermatitis, and dementia. More than half of the severe cases died and estimates of milder attacks ranged in the hundreds of thousands.

He soon knew that several medical theories were wrong. Pellagra was not caused by too much sun, corn rot or a certain microbe. Surely he must have been viewed as a "mad scientist" when he set about to prove his convictions that pellagra was not infectious by injecting himself with blood taken from a person in the acute stages of pellagra. Moreover, his wife and associates, heroines and heroes all, allowed him to inject them also! He went so far as to make capsules from skin scrapings and fecal material of pellagra victims. Then he swallowed the capsules.

Goldberger theorized that an important food nutrient was missing. He called this unknown substance the "pellagra-preventative factor". In experiments with prison inmates and orphans in Mississippi, he found that a diet which included lean meat, milk, eggs and yeast cured the pitiable victims. As to the exact missing chemical, Goldberger tested his theory of this deficiency in 1922 with outstanding results, aware that the mysterious factor was an amino acid. (Oddly, he and his associate, Tanner, did not report these findings.) But the data he and his associates amassed have been used to determine human requirement for nicotinic acid even though this vitamin was unknown in his lifetime.

Goldberger, during his dangerous career, worked his way up to be head of the pathology department at National Institutes of Health. He contracted typhus, yellow fever and the dreaded dengue (an infectious tropical disease of the back and joints).

Dr. James Leake told the story about the time Dr. McCoy assigned Dr. Kenneth Maxcy to research Dengue fever in Alabama and Georgia. Upon returning to Washington, D.C. Dr. Maxcy reported orally to the (medical) Journal Club. He discussed cases which showed an agglutination with certain proteins, called a Weil-Felix reaction. Dr. Goldberger spoke up. "Why isn't this typhus?" Dr. Maxcy returned to the south and subsequently proved that the disease was typhus and not dengue.

When, in the late 1920's Dr. Goldberger became very ill with cancer, he checked in at the Naval Hospital. (Alice would be treated at this nearby hospital which, in fact, was separated from the Hygienic Laboratory by only a garden wall.) There Goldberger received two whole blood transfusions each day from devoted laboratory medical officers who lay, one on each side of him, and transfused their blood directly. Knowing that he was dying, Goldberger instructed three close friends, Dr. McCoy, who was director of National Institutes of Health at that time, Assistant Surgeon General Dr. Arthur Stimson, and Dr. James Leake, to arrange for his cremation. Afterwards, in a simple ceremony, they released the ashes in the Potomac River.

Sadly, they discovered later, Goldberger's wife and children were left with little money. Soon, a bill was introduced and passed in the federal legislature ordering the Mrs. Goldberger receive a pension of 125 dollars a month, higher than other government investigative widows received, because she had taken a life-risking part in her husband's experiments.

Courageous Joseph Goldberger, bacteriologist and epidemiologist, a man of acute intellectual insight "...illuminated everything he touched and won the admiration and affection of his associates," Dr. Arthur Stimson wrote. Alice, who devoted a paragraph to Goldberger in her autobiography, must have known him, followed his career and rejoiced with him in his breakthroughs.

Another medical doctor with the Hygienic Laboratory, R.R. Spencer (nicknamed "Spenny"), was assigned to work with Rocky Mountain spotted fever. A Virginian, Hollywood handsome, with a small mustache and large, dark eyes, Spenny and his team pursued this terrible disease, sometimes called "black measles."

It is a disease of nature, meaning that the organism which causes human sickness normally lives in wild animals. Its name is <u>Rickettsia rickettsii</u> and it occurs only in the western hemisphere. It is an extremely tiny bacterium that lives within the cells of the host, a trait held by viruses but very few bacteria. Wood ticks are its host. These insects then bite mammals, including human, causing the disease, spotted fever. Although scientists first thought that Rocky Mountain spotted fever, with its extensive rash, fever, harsh joint and muscle pain, was a western United States disease, it occurs everywhere in the country.

It had cost the lives of several researchers before Spenny and entomologist, Dr. R.R. Parker, (called the two

R.R.'s) teamed up to work both early and late at a branch laboratory, an old two-story schoolhouse in Hamilton, Montana. They eventually formulated a vaccine against spotted fever using ground-up ticks.

A kindly "pack rat" who could not bear to discard anything he had used in experiments, Dr. Spencer earned considerable fame for this life-saving vaccine.

Chapter 9

Dangerous Microbes

"Courage – fear that has said its prayers."
— Dorothy Bernard

The summer of 1918 came and went; Alice faced the meningitis problem each morning with serenity. Soon she would know this period as the lull before the worst storm of disease our country had ever suffered.

During a hot autumn afternoon the city of Washington, D.C. began taking to its sick bed. Each day added more victims. They lay in all stages of severity until they either got well or died. Influenza!

Folks called this disease the "flu" or the "grippe." What doctors didn't know then, was that influenza is caused by a virus so small it could not be seen with the microscopes then available to them. When the electron microscope came out of Germany 19 years later, medical science leaped into a new, brightly-lighted world of disease diagnosis.

Influenza had raced through Europe, hit Massachusetts in September, and within three weeks besieged Washingtonians. A great number of women, having come to take war-time work, became infected because of overcrowded housing conditions. Three and four persons shared a room meant for one. Sadly, any person who came down with the "flu" became an immediate outcast. Some landladies sent away roomers who appeared to have the disease.

Congress quickly passed a resolution giving the Public Heath Service permission and means to fight this "Spanish influenza" and any other communicable diseases. This meant that state and local boards could ask for assistance from the federal government.

The disease attacked anyone who could not ward off its infectious nature. Thousands died in the Washington area. At the height of the outbreak, families burying their dead had to give up graveside services due to traffic jams caused by funeral processions in the cemeteries!

The Hygienic Laboratory sprang into action. Medical officers rushed out of Washington to assist state and local health departments. Doctors involved in research put away their tools and charts and returned to medical practice, caring for ill government workers. Others set up emergency hospitals. Between sick personnel and the absence of doctors, the Hygienic Laboratory became an abandoned place. Alice thus far had escaped the disease. She continued her meningitis experimentation. In mid-October Dr. McCoy stopped by her work-station. Waving his hands in his own characteristic way, he told her, "Alice, I must ask you to drop your current problem. We have a subject of greatest concern with the 'influenza bacillus'. We need you on this."

"Of course", Alice said, her mind racing. A new challenge! Alice's thoughts charged about in a dozen directions at once. She folded her arms across her breast and looked up into the worried face of her beloved chief. McCoy smiled, knowing she had sprung far beyond this moment in her mind.

"I can examine sputum of patients and autopsy tissues." Softly, almost dreamily, she added, "Perhaps I can find the dominating bacterial species."

McCoy nodded, wheeled and trotted away down the aisle of the old room, his suit coat unbuttoned and flapping.

Alice set out immediately for the media room. Because the media-maker was ill, she would have to make a special culture medium, something she had not done for herself in a long time. Alice hoped fervently she would be able to remember the procedure and carry on the enormous task she had agreed to undertake.

She plunged into the procedure, and within minutes, knew she was doing poorly. Her memory of the method was sharp but her hands fumbled, refused to obey. Nothing was going right. A wave of helplessness swept over her. She felt weak and headachey. She set down the utensils and leaned against the counter, not wanting to believe the symptoms. She had the "flu."

Slowly and methodically, Alice, trembling, returned all the equipment to its place. Then she walked home and fell into bed.

Alice was ill with the "Spanish influenza" for a month. Doctors from the Hygienic Laboratory visited, treating her with laxatives and fruit juices, especially hot lemonade, and steamy foot baths made from mustard powder. They ordered her to stay in bed but permitted her to get up to eat and take care of personal needs. While Alice suffered from the typical fever, chills, joint ache and coughing, the epidemic worsened.

Dr. McCoy took care of the Laboratory's uncomplicated "flu" cases and continued, miraculously, to run the administrative part of the institute. Dr. Leake cared for the severe illnesses, which had turned into pneumonia, bronchitis, sinus and mastoid infections. They were housed in temporary hospitals.

By the time Alice returned to work, it was November, 1918, World War I was over, the Allies had won the war, and Armistice Day had been celebrated. She picked up her delayed <u>meningococcol</u> work and on this project received the go-ahead to experiment with small rodents, a procedure which she previously had to ask another department to do. The influenza left Alice a bit wobbly at first and she fatigued easily but in time her natural good health prevailed.

She was lucky. Throughout our planet, some 20 million persons had died of influenza. She could not know that the world would wait another 15 years before an investigating team in England proved that the cause of all the many kinds of influenza was a virus.

Alice picked up her work where she had dropped it when illness struck. Yet she clung to her interest in Mediterranean-Malta-fever (which in 1913 had its name officially changed to undulant fever.) During her early years at the Hygienic Laboratory, Alice did not identify and investigate much of the history of this disease which would be called by its scientific name, brucellosis. Now, in

1919, there would be time to dig into the old, as well as the recent, research.

She could not have dreamed of the frustration and anguish she would endure as distinguished medical men disputed her speech and the subsequent publication in the scientific journal relating her discovery of the twin microbes. They questioned her ability and her integrity. Men who had invested in the dairy industry even suggested Alice had made deals with the manufacturers of pasteurization equipment!

Pushing aside the attacks, Alice determined to dig up as much information about Bang's disease as was available. We recall her discovery that the germ causing Bang's disease in cattle belonged to the same family as the bacteria found in goat's milk, which caused undulant fever in humans.

Alice collected and pored over literature about diseased goats in the southwest United States. Scientists in Great Britain and France had published many papers on this subject. One fact became clear to her. Undulant fever was being confused with other common diseases like typhoid fever, tuberculosis and malaria. With the name officially changed to undulant fever, more complications evolved. The typically up-and-down-fever curve in humans us; ally appeared in severe cases only. How could the sickness be called undulant fever if the temperature did not undulate? Again, she decided, in the milder cases it was misdiagnosed.

Going deeper and farther back in the disease's history, Alice read with relish the report of the British Dr. M.L. Hughes. He cared for sick service men on duty during the War in Crimea (a peninsula in southern Russia) which ended in 1856. In his classic of medical literature, Hughes said that it was "common" to find Crimean War veterans diagnosed as having rheumatism, following attacks of chronic undulant fever. He defended the men, saying they were not pretending to be ill in order to collect pensions or for any other reason.

Alice delighted in reading about another British medical army officer and his wife. His pockets almost empty, David Bruce had joined the army in 1884 because he wanted to get married and the 1,000 dollars-a-year salary looked good. His country had an armed forces base in Malta, south of Italy in the Mediterranean Sea. The little island was part of Great Britain's imperial system which supported a medical corps. The corps produced outstanding research, a prime example being the discovery that mosquitoes carry malaria.

At this time there was a deadly outbreak of "Mediterranean-Malta fever" among the enlisted men as well as the civilian population. David received orders to report to Malta to tackle the fever problem. Immediately he and his bride, Mary, set sail for Malta. The journey became their honeymoon.

Bruce, a physician, and his microscopist wife had hardly stepped off the boat when they saw the gravity of the "Malta fever" problem. The base hospital was filled with suffering men and the deadhouse doors opened and shut too often.

David's instructions had been to minister to the stricken soldiers on the island. He dutifully set out making rounds and learning about the disease. Because the emerging science of bacteriology was yet primitive, physicians had no way of knowing the origin of Malta fever. They simply treated outstanding symptoms.

Mary Bruce encouraged, then begged, her husband to

search for the cause of this disease until he agreed. Each morning he buttoned a cool work shirt over his huge chest, combed his droopy mustache and headed for a small derelict building where they had made a laboratory. It wasn't much, for neither of them had had training other than basic culture making, a fact that did not hinder their devotion, once they became intrigued with Malta fever. Pasteur and Koch's new germ theory, that of identifying a certain microorganism to be the cause of a distinct infectious disease and following up with documentation of pathological changes, would soon overthrow medical scientists' old ideas.

Mary Bruce toiled over her crude microscope. She held David's experimental and uncooperative monkeys when he injected or examined them. (They cost $1.75 each, bought with the Bruces' own money). She made notes, observations and drawings related to Malta fever. British army officers and their wives at the remote post spoke of Mary's devotion to her husband and the project in which the couple collaborated so closely. They did not perceive her as a scientist; she was that tiny Mrs. Bruce who seemed to be inseparable from her husband, at work or otherwise.

The long-sought breakthrough came in 1886 (about the time young Alice was battling scarlet fever, perhaps) when they received tissue from the spleen of a soldier who had died of Malta fever. The young couple worked continually; they fired each other's desire to find the cause of the misery-laden disease. Because it was new territory they had innumerable setbacks. "My plan has been a washout," David groaned when they had to rework experiments dozens of times, ending without any answers.

They persevered. To their advantage was the year-around pleasant weather. When the ramshackle laboratory became too frustrating, they could play lawn tennis, go boating or take tea with their friends. Then one day Mary Bruce cultivated the bacillus which was the source of the fever! The origin seemed to be infected goats.

The Bruces checked the milk of the island's goat herd and found that "their micrococcus" showed up in one-fifth of the samples. David, with great joy and satisfaction, quickly ordered all raw goat's milk consumption stopped within the garrison and new cases of Malta fever nearly disappeared.

He gave the wrong generic name, Micrococcus, to their discovery. It was an excusable mistake, Alice wrote later, because bacteriology was a new science. True, David had studied to be a surgeon under Dr. Robert Koch in Berlin, Germany, but that had been in the era before Dr. Koch founded the science that would lead to miraculous discoveries of cures and vaccines for dreaded diseases.

Ironically, the Bruces were sent to Africa to study the tsetse fly disease before they could do much follow-up work with their discovery. The English Army medical officers cared little for David and Mary's consuming interest in Malta fever. In 1888 the disappointed couple boarded a ship, headed on to sleeping sickness territory in Africa. David was being transferred. They returned in June of 1904, and this time David was the chairman of the Royal Society Subcommittee on Mediterranean fever. He promptly took up studies of M. melitensis in goats and humans.

Around 1930 the tropical disease from Malta would be officially named brucellosis in David Bruce's honor. Mary Bruce deserved credit for much of the discovery, yet in his celebrated report to the commission, her husband did not even once mention her name! The British government eventually heaped honors upon him, and Mary as his wife (but not research partner) was given the title "Lady Bruce". Alice must have understood Mary Bruce's feelings when she, Alice, claimed the answer to the second part of the Malta fever mystery.

Discovery Number One then was a bacterium from the milk of infected goats that caused undulant fever in humans, as proved by the Bruces. Discovery Number Two, the germ found in cow's milk is related to the germ in goat's milk. Discovery Number Three: both cause undulant fever in humans! Alice proved this, 30 years later.

Just as Mary Bruce waited a long time to be recognized for her contribution – the first Honorary female member of the Royal Microscopical Society – so Alice had to wait for recognition of her revelation, quietly fighting the powerful men in science and industry who discredited her laboratory work.

How Alice Catherine Evans did so is the remainder of this story.

****

Chapter 10

Enter The Enemy

"You gain strength, courage and confidence by every experience in which you really stop to look fear in the face..."
- Eleanor Roosevelt

Alice's work with cow (bovine) diseases, as related to human illness, led her toward publications about typhoid outbreaks and tuberculosis. She found that as early as 1900, some authorities had said that human tuberculosis could be caused by the bovine organism.

The next year, however, the famous German physician, Robert Koch, declared that bovine tuberculosis could not infect humans. The medical world accepted Koch's belief, having no reason not to. After all, Robert Koch developed the revolutionary process of incubating, staining and growing microorganisms, a technique which remains the basis for studying bacteriological infections today. By 1876, he had created an inoculation method using Pasteur's anthrax serum which prevented this ghastly cattle disease. He discovered the tuberculosis-causing germ which is still sometimes called "the Koch bacillus." He identified, for the first time, the microbe responsible for Asiatic cholera. In Africa, he researched blood infections and sleeping sickness, and after sailing to India he studied bubonic plague.

The balding, bearded man with the gold, oval eyeglasses perched on his nose won the Nobel Prize in 1905 for his tuberculosis work. Before he died in 1910, Koch had invented dry heat sterilization. But Koch's declaration that it wasn't necessary to protect humans from cattle tuberculosis certainly did not accelerate progress in fighting this common disease.

Alice, the bacteriologist, gave this outstanding researcher full credit for his wonderful accomplishments. Alice, the researcher, in possibly the greatest understatement of her career, wrote, "But even Koch could make mistakes."

Yet we know that the certified milk movement was alive and kicking up a fuss. Its members believed correctly, in spite of the eminent doctor's views, that tuberculosis could be transmitted by cows. Truly, the certification rules were a blessing in regard to tuberculosis infection. But other organisms, which eventually would be called brucella, were a different breed, a kind that could not be controlled by certification standards.

When Alice worked for the Dairy Division of the Department of Agriculture, she concentrated on identifying infectious organisms from milk products. Researchers pressed forward, assuming that raw, fresh milk, having no obvious contaminants, was safe to drink. Alice now spent interminable but productive hours with her nose stuck in laboratory reports from those early years of the decade.

She found that, in 1906, during a six-month period, the District of Columbia (Washington, D.C., area) had three distinct outbreaks of typhoid fever. The chief of the Hygienic Laboratory had drawn up an intensive census of where patients lived, and the severity of their ailments. Of the 866 cases, 85 of them were traced to drinking infected milk! The report said the ingested milk was, "for the most part, too old, too dirty and too warm." It had passed through... "too many hands" and was ripe for pollution.

The report went on to detail connections between infected milk and the little food markets. In these "Mom and Pop" stores the same hands that tended sick family members in the house next to the store also handled the raw milk. Flies buzzed everywhere.

These scenes, played all over the world, made diseases like scarlet fever, diphtheria and typhoid fever frightful household words. Everyone recognized the bright-colored quarantine signs that the Department of Health workers nailed to the houses where these infections made hostages of the victims. Milk, of course, was only one source of spreading disease.

Incredibly, as far back as 1892, a far-sighted, charitable man, who happened to be very rich, distributed coal, food and pasteurized milk to the desperate poor in New York City. Nathan Straus also established pasteurized milk stations in 35 other cities in our country. And it was free to all takers!

Within the next 28 years, while medical officials still hung back and there were few laws to sanitize raw milk, this wonderful Jewish man financed the building of 297 pasteurized milk-distribution depots, both abroad and in the U.S. Straus was an immigrant and part-owner of R.H. Macy and Co. (Macy's Department Store). Because of his special compassion for children, the infant mortality rate dropped greatly within the pockets of poverty. How he happened to believe in pasteurization is another story. Wasn't it ironic that many destitute families living in the Straus milk depot areas were saved from disease and death, whereas more prosperous families, drinking "certified milk", innocently gambled with their families' health and lives?

Alice now worked full-time on samples of infected milk, caused by diseased udders in cows. At first she suspected tuberculosis to be the source of infection. In parts of the United States, 30% of these infected cows actually had sores on the udders, yet this milk was sold. Health authorities ignored the poisonous amounts of tubercle bacilli this milk contained. After all, wasn't it well-known that cattle tuberculosis could not infect humans?

Dr. Theobald Smith, when Alice was yet a girl in her teens, disputed the "fact" that there was only one type of tubercle bacillus. He stated that although there were differences in the human and bovine cultures, they were related. They could be dangerous to humans, he wrote. This announcement was to become an intriguing but baffling puzzle to Alice in later years.

Turning farther back in history, to 1900, Alice pinpointed several papers which told about butchers or veterinarians contracting tuberculosis after dissecting an infected animal.

Family doctors began to report minor outbreaks – several members of a household, children at school, or a ward of infants in a hospital suddenly developing intestinal tuberculosis. Evidence accumulated. Cows supplying milk for these persons turned out to be in advanced state of tuberculosis. We remember that by 1907, the U.S. Public Health Service went on record as saying that pasteurization was the only way to eliminate milk as a carrier of "common communicable diseases." It was a suggestion, a warning. The Commission of Milk Standards in 1910, drew up guidelines for all market milk. They stopped short of insisting on pasteurization because they believed that following these standards for animal and human health inspections was sufficient to prevent infectious germs from contaminating dairy products.

But Alice realized, as she scanned the old records, there was no provision for the possibility that healthy-looking animals might be diseased. It could be, for example, that a cow might pick up infection right after it was examined and tested. The milk, then, would be diseased, spreading infection and misery to consumers until the next testing.

Alice was disturbed; no laws backed up the commission. She had to take comfort when milk for the military, by law, was pasteurized in 1917.

Alice did not invest much energy fretting about the controversy. She pressed on with other research assignments, keeping the undulant fever discovery in the back room of her mind. Often, though, Dr. Smith brought the subject to the front with his repeated "strong opposition" to Alice's view that brucellosis can be transmitted from animals to humans.

Why did Theobald Smith take this position? Why did this German immigrant's son, who was described as being the "most distinguished early American microbiologist and probably the leading comparative pathologist in the world" never ask for a professional meeting with Alice? What progress they might have initiated on the long bumpy road to victory over undulant fever, if they had met earlier in the controversy.

Surely Smith's beginnings were as humble as Alice's. His father was a tailor; his mother took in boarders in Albany, New York. A shy lad, with beautiful dark eyes, his self discipline, hard-driving work habits and superb talent for scientific studies caught the attention of Burt Wilder at Cornell University, the same eccentric genius Alice was to study under years later. Wilder mentored Theobald, who graduated in 1877 and went on to medical school.

Upon finishing requirements, Smith told colleagues he felt unready to hang up his sign as a doctor. He accepted a job in the Department of Agriculture, in the new Bureau of Animal Industry. In 1886 he pioneered studies in hog cholera and brilliantly designed a new program for bacterial vaccine production. In the following years, Smith's superior officers repeatedly took credit for his work, or attributed his successes to other researchers. Even the far-famed Dr. Robert Koch privately confirmed Smith's remarkable observations on tubercle bacilli, then waited ten years to announce Smith's authorship.

This bearded man with regular, almost classical facial lines, could not be held back in the shadows forever. His research continued to be outstanding. Dr. Hans Zinsser, who did such remarkable pioneer research in rickettsial disease that a subgenus of this microbe was named after him, became Alice's valued friend. Zinsser said "there was about him(Smith) an unobtrusive pride, a reserve tinged with austerity which did not invite easy intimacy."

Smith grew to be "held in profound admiration", the

Dictionary of Scientific Biography says of him. "Too reticent to be popular..., but fair in judgment."

"Fair in judgment!" What happened to cause Theobald Smith to disallow Alice, a sister scientist, her views? Had he not suffered the same injustices? Could he have been 'getting even' at the powerful men who betrayed him? Or maybe he had a deep-seated bias against a woman in the workplace, especially one who did not have a medical degree.

She smarted but didn't let it affect her work. At this time, 1920, Alice again began to scour scientific journals for data about undulant fever. She pin-pointed a paper by Dr. Karl Meyer in San Francisco who wrote of his research linking undulant fever to contagious abortion in cows.

Confirmations like these gave Alice the strength and patience to keep faith in herself. Two years later, in Phoenix, Arizona, an outbreak of undulant fever began, for her, a journey toward the truth; the "event for which I had been waiting," Alice said.

The victims had fallen sick with the disease during the summer. A few of them were recovering from tuberculosis when they came down with undulant fever. Two of them died. A physician from the Hygienic Laboratory hurriedly packed his bag and rode the train to Phoenix to help prevent the epidemic from spreading. He mailed back cultures taken from patients as well as those from goat's milk, the likely carrier.

Alice's spirits rose; here were 35 diagnosed, confirmed cases of undulant fever! Not that she lacked compassion for the unfortunate patients; soon she would find out first-hand the anguish caused by this germ. What she saw presented in this southwestern tragedy was a stage setting for the drama that Alice had written in her head these past nine years.

Yet she did not have free rein, emotionally, to charge ahead with the research. In July of 1920, her father died. It was not unexpected but Alice felt a profound loss. So much of what I am and whatever I've accomplished I owe to him, Alice thought, as she slipped into a black dress and prepared to travel back to Pennsylvania. There, she helped settle her father's meager estate, stored his stout wooden cane and gave away his old wool suits.

Soon after, Alice's mother, Annie, went to live with Morgan and his young family in North Ridgeville, Ohio. Annie looked older than her years, with a complexion deeply creased by a farm wife's exposure to sun and wind. Her granddaughter, Sarah Jeannette, Morgan's last-born child, remembered her as "a rather stern person," a recollection from the perception of a four-year-old child.

Alice, however, could trace to this serious-minded lady much of her own sense of self-worth and determination. Certainly, if Annie had not pitched in, earned extra money for her children's education, worked on the farm as hard as any man, treated her growing daughter with respect, this story of Alice would not be written.

Morgan's wife, Zoe, then had a three-generation household. Little Sarah had an older sister, Anna, and a brother, Marvin. When Sarah was four, Annie moved to the Elyria Home for the Aged where she quietly lived out her few remaining months. Dispirited, Alice and Morgan arranged to have their mother's remains sent back to Neath and buried next to their father's grave.

After her father's funeral Alice had immersed herself in the Phoenix culture study, and identified the strain as <u>M.</u>

<u>melitensis</u>, typical of caprine or goat infections.

Dr. McCoy wisely gave Alice other projects. With Sally Branham, she would later spend much time toiling on meningococci, and with Ida Bengtson, she shared a work load on the study of clostridia toxins. It was an inspired directive, for these three women became lifelong friends.

Soon after she picked up the Phoenix project, in the mail came something that would spark her energies and lead her back to undulant fever research. The return address read, "Dr. Harold Amoss, John Hopkins Hospital, Baltimore, Maryland." Dr. Amoss wanted to know whether the enclosed bacterial strain was from cow or goat. He had taken it from a hospital patient.

When Alice completed the agglutinin-absorption test, she stood rooted to the worn wooden floor. She felt as though she had been plugged into an electric current. The strain was <u>Bacillus abortus</u>! The breakthrough!

In other words, Alice had living, microscopic proof that <u>B. abortus</u> could be carried from cow to a human. This was the first instance in the United States in which undulant fever in a human could be traced directly to cattle and not the goat strain, <u>M. melitensis</u>.

"The finding of the Baltimore case of brucellosis, the first not of caprine (goat) origin in this country, and the recovery of the causal organism from the patient, impelled me to resume the study of brucellosis in earnest…"

Chapter 11

Carrying On

"If I felt it was the right thing to do, I was for it, regardless of the possible outcome..."
- Golda Meir

Humming to herself, Alice headed for Dr. McCoy's office, her mind racing forward, devising ways to restart her brucellosis study. The chief's face lit up when she recounted her breakthrough. With his blessing and wings on her feet, Alice floated back to her work station.

The euphoria was not to last. Sometime between summer and fall, when Alice had handled the Phoenix and Baltimore cultures, she had become infected with the goat bacteria, <u>melitensis</u>. Bacteriologists did not know that ordinary precautions, such as they took for common typhoid fever or meningitis, were no guarantee against this microbe. Alice, of course, understood that she labored in "dangerous work". She exercised extreme caution. Yet these germs, which would be known as brucellae, could move through air and had claimed Alice when she breathed them in. Unaware that she carried an incubating germ, Alice pursued the reopened project with passion.

"One day," Alice wrote in her memoirs, "the subject of human brucella infection was under discussion with Dr. McCoy and a few other medical officers of the Laboratory. The suggestion was made by Dr. Walter T. Harrison that there was one more experiment that should be carried out which might strengthen the evidence of a close relationship between the causal organisms of bovine contagious abortion and human undulant fever..."

"I think a pregnant cow should be inoculated with M. melitensis (goat brucellae)," he said.

Alice felt a sudden hot, galvanizing wave of hope wash through her, but she held her voice steady. "I agree. Do you think that such an arrangement can be carried out?"

McCoy nodded. "I believe so. Let me see what I can do at the Bureau of Animal Industry," he said.

Shortly afterwards, an apprehensive Alice accompanied Dr. McCoy to a farmhouse in Chevy Chase, Maryland, close to the corner of Wisconsin Avenue and Bradley Boulevard. It had been converted to a laboratory for pathologists of the Bureau. She need not have fretted, for these doctors "cheerfully and willingly" carried out Alice's experiment. They expressed the same unbelief, however, that she had heard from their colleagues 6 years earlier. One of the pathologists shook his head. "I don't think anything is going to happen," he said.

Alice handed him the syringe of goat brucellae, hesitating only a moment. If he could be candid, so could she.

"I expect something is going to happen," she said.

Something did happen. Forty-six days after inoculation, the cow lost the calf by miscarriage. When the pathologists analyzed the fetus, M. melitensis showed up in the stomach and other fluids. It was present, too, in the cow's first milk.

Here was more proof! Goat strains and cow strains of the brucella organism produced the same results in experimental animals. Oh, life was sweet! Never mind those afternoons when she got so tired and achey she could hardly pick up a flask. Success drew out her physical reserves; she began a huge project, one using 500 samples of human blood her own laboratory had secured to test for another disease. Using these remnants, she added to the experiment blood samples from a nearby Naval Hospital and other veterans' hospital specimens. It was tedious work but she plowed methodically through the procedures.

Without warning, it materialized before her eyes. One of the samples reacted positively to B. abortus! Furthermore, doctors at the Navel Hospital confirmed Alice's finding.

They quickly located the donor. In Alice's words…"the ambulatory patient, secretary to a congressman, lived in suburban Virginia and was in the habit of drinking raw cow's milk. This was the second case of human brucellosis not traceable to goats to be recognized in this country; it was the FIRST in which the evidence pointed toward cow's milk as the source of infection."

A goal reached, a dream realized, but Alice, after the initial thrill, found that Dr. Smith, in a distant laboratory, worked with equal dedication to prove her wrong. He would be a powerful enemy.

Finally, the incubating germ inside Alice's small body made itself known. Alice began to have symptoms of what

100

appeared to be influenza. She was desperately tired. Her joints pained. She reported each morning to the old red building, but she walked home more slowly, felt chilly more often and shook with fever at night. She had thought, "I must take my temperature." In the freshness of daylight, she felt rested and forgot to use the thermometer. Before the clock indicated her lunch hour, she was usually ill again. She plodded through the afternoon hours and it was all she could manage to tidy her workplace at quitting time.

In spite of her training, Alice allowed herself to be lulled into apathy. The symptoms are out-of-sequence, she told herself. If it is brucellosis, shouldn't the acute illness start the phase, followed by minor, chronic sickness?

When the acute fever struck, Alice knew, both in head and heart, she had undulant fever. The fever dropped; climbed to a higher peak and dropped again. "Each wave," Alice said, "was worse than the preceding." Knife-like pains attacked her joints; some struck so brutally it took away her breath.

Unable to function, Alice dragged herself to a laboratory doctor.

Quickly installed in Johns Hopkins Hospital, she languished for 10 weeks.

****

As she rested quietly in the narrow bed, Alice reflected on the development of the illness that had placed her in the

Baltimore hospital. She remembered grubbing through the meningitis assignment, and becoming beastly tired and out-of-sorts before each day ended. Yet it didn't seem right that she should whine about it, with her colleagues falling and sometimes dying from handling dangerous microbes.

She moved her throbbing joints carefully to a sitting position and wondered about the precisely crafted scientific paper she had sent to the World Dairy Congress. She had drafted a colleague to read it in her absence. The dairymen were assembled, that October of 1923, in Syracuse, New York. She knew the essay by heart, particularly the crucial words that should challenge the milk producers. "It would appear to be a problem worthy of investigation to determine whether <u>abortus</u> infection might not be responsible for mild disabilities in our own localities, for the cause is never determined..." and in conclusion, "If there were no other reasons for milk pasteurization, it would appear to be folly to drink raw milk containing <u>abortus</u> organisms."

Alice dared to hope her words would be taken seriously; reality told her they would not be. The listening men earned a prosperous living with methods they had been told were safe and healthy. Why should they pay attention to an unknown bacteriologist who accused them of selling disease-ridden milk to their customers?

****

Chapter 12

Unexpected Partner

> *"Put in your oar, and share the*
> *sweat of the brow with which you*
> *must start up the stream..."*
> - Elizabeth Phelps

Alice came home with no name to call her illness. This first attack was the only one to fit the description of undulant fever, yet doctors declined to diagnose it, preferring, instead, to write, "neurasthenia" on her medical record. This was medical jargon for persons with "imaginary or pretended ills."

Alice was too weak to do more than feel outraged. Much later, she wrote, "To be ill and regarded as an impostor is to be in an almost intolerable situation, and a damaged reputation is not easily repaired. The rule of law that a suspect should be considered innocent until guilt is proved ought to be applied in medicine." Later she would rally to the defense of others labeled with the tag, "neurasthenia". For the present, this year of 1923, Alice had to let go of her reasonable wish for diagnosis. Her illness hung unnamed even as she checked out of the hospital and returned to work.

There she noticed, Pooler, her helper, seemed to be drooping. Yes, he felt poorly, he told Alice.

Alice promptly sent him to a lab medical doctor to have blood drawn. She went along, too, and had a sample of hers taken to use as a "normal" or control specimen. She knew, of course, that she had accidentally infected herself with brucella. She shrugged it off. Wasn't it better to hope she would have a light case of undulant fever and be more perceptive of her health in the future? Perhaps she would revive in the joy of being once more with her laboratory family!

She worried about Pooler. He might be coming down with a dangerous microbe. Alice was surprised, then alarmed, when she ran the tests. Pooler was just a little under the weather. No infections. Then the shocker. Her own blood, the control sample, tested positive for undulant fever! The titer was not high enough to be significant, but Alice "wondered what it might mean." In spite of its being slightly below the level that meant undoubted brucellar infection, couldn't it be there was a *DEGREE* of infection present?

Confirming her own diagnosis wasn't much comfort. It came to Alice, ironically, that she had been quoted as saying, ... "in general, the bovine abortus does not cause in man such an acute disease as the Malta fever of subtropical

104

regions…"

How true! Alice had this goat disease, "Malta fever," or undulant fever, and she herself would be the only one sure about the identity of her illness for many years to come.

Alice endured. She had good days, not-so-fine-days and days when she couldn't raise her head from the pillow. On one of the good days, at her laboratory, fortune visited in the person of Dr. Charles Carpenter. On this bleak winter afternoon in 1925, some two years after her hospitalization, this young man would seem to refute Alice's words in the story he brought, as well as with the blood cultures he carefully placed on her workbench. He was a nice, plain-looking young man, with brown hair, and intelligent gray eyes which looked through small eyeglasses at his scientific world. And what a world he saw! Charles had earned two doctor's degrees, one as a specialist in treating horses, the other in bacteriology.

He came from Cornell University because he heard about Alice C. Evans and her research. He confessed this research was not in his job description. But, he said, his eyes shining, he just knew he was on to something that might save two critically ill boys whose symptoms shouted undulant fever.

Intrigued, Alice questioned him about the cultures and blood samples he handled as if they were jewels.

Carpenter explained that the specimens came from two lads, students at Cornell University, who were, at times, near death. They had temperatures which almost soared off the chart and the shaking chills. Doctors guessed at diagnoses, suggesting everything from malaria and blood poisoning, to streptococcus and tuberculosis.

As a pathologist, Carpenter was allowed to draw blood samples from the boys' arms. Then, he said, he had dashed to the laboratory to plant microbes on food samples. Smiling, he told Alice how he had babied the cultures, until he had - and here he paused for effect - an undulant fever microbe. Both boys were infected with it.

Carpenter revealed to Alice, shyly, that he had followed her progress with diligence, and he was there to ask a favor, to learn from her. Would she honor him by doing the lab test, the one that shows whether the microbe is Bang or Bruce?

Alice agreed with a modest smile. The man had two medical degrees, had come all the way from Ithaca, New York, and was treating her like a prophet. Without wasting a motion, she put away her work-in-progress and set up materials for typing the samples. Carpenter hovered about, greatly curious.

When it was done, the vigorous "horse doctor" hopped the train at the Washington station, planning with delectation what he would do for the hospitalized boys upon arriving back at the university.

Once there, Carpenter rushed to the dairy barns that furnished the university with fresh, raw milk. These were "certified" healthy cows, and the milk was produced under the most sanitary conditions. He made himself unpopular by taking samples from each classy purebred cow. College officials knew he was searching for a place to assign the guilt for the boys' disease - whatever it was. And the administrators as well as the medical doctors resented his interference. Like Alice, he was criticized; unlike Alice, he was not ignored. He was, after all, a man and a doctor.

Mixing these milk samples into a solution, he injected

guinea pigs. Within a month the animals died from <u>Br. abortus</u>! He had confirmed, with Alice's help, and in her words, "the first case of human brucellosis in this country in which a culture was obtained (directly) from a patient and the infection was traced to cow's milk..."

Carpenter notified the hospital and the patients. Then, his energies in high gear, he poked, snooped and pried into all the human cases he could locate which had symptoms of the Bang infection. He found 17 persons in Ithaca alone who had this microbe in their blood. All these city dwellers drank raw milk, except one. That patient was a bacteriologist who had worked with the bacillus.

Local doctors stopped making fun of Carpenter, and began to "discover" patients with undulant fever symptoms. They were people from every economic status. Dr. Carpenter determined that people showing no outward sign of the Bang-Bruce disease could be harboring it within their bodies, and he proved it by a blood test. He found one of the twin microbes in the first fatal human case in America; the mother aborted spontaneously and the baby died. How many other mothers drinking raw cow's milk, he asked, had already miscarried their babies?

With his assistant, Ruth Boak, who intermittently suffered with undulant fever contracted as a student at Cornell, from the same "healthy" herd of cows that had nearly killed the two sick boys, Carpenter kept digging away at the problem. He isolated cases of this fever in people who were being treated for tuberculosis in a sanitarium. They, too, had drunk raw cow's milk. After pasteurization was instituted in this area there were no new cases.

Gratified that she no longer had to fight the medical and

dairy establishment alone, Alice concentrated on picking up her career and restoring herself to good health. "During those nine and the following years," she said, "short hospital experiences were too numerous to be recalled...The exacerbation of 1923 was the only one that resembled the description of "undulant fever." As in many cases of chronic brucellosis, there were no clinical signs of disease during the long periods of ill health, and I was in a first-rate situation for repeated diagnosis of neurasthenia, with its implications of malingering. That was my fate until May, 1928, when another disease intervened which required surgery. The impasse was broken when lesions were found from which <u>Br. melitensis</u> was cultivated. Thus, accidentally at last, came relief from the misunderstandings which will arise inevitably when a patient is told that he is suffering from imaginary or pretended ills." Alice savored the news, however accidental. It freed her forever from the humiliating medical stigma.

****

Alice had delved, in the years between 1918 and 1928, into the study of brucellosis. Every spare minute at work, and evenings at home in her easy chair or at a small table Alice searched through medical literature from all parts of the world. Dr. Theobald Smith persisted, too. Word drifted back to Alice that the eminent medical man continued his research on brucellae. Alice watched for and read his published reports on brucellosis of cattle. They appeared in 1919 and 1925. She expected them, somehow, to refute her finding, but nothing new came out of his work. The doctor's viewpoint, of course had not changed. Alice, then, was not surprised when a colleague told her Dr. Smith felt so strongly about the subject, that whenever the topic came up in conversation, he declared he intended to disprove Alice's discovery.

Anyone would have reason to be intimidated by this prominent man's onslaught. Dr. Smith had a brilliant record. He climbed from the Bureau of Animal Industry to a professorship at Harvard Medical School, then on to Directorship of the Department of Animal Pathology at Rockefeller Institute. Probably his greatest achievement was his work with Texas cattle fever. He found that infected ticks transmitted the disease. This discovery was one of the first indications that insects can carry disease. Furthermore, he contributed with distinction to the understanding of other diseases, especially tuberculosis.

Alice continued to hear, from various sources, about Dr. Smith's hostility. It worried her. She would have been less than human if she did not feel a certain amount of personal insult. She put science first, however, and believed, without a qualm, that brucellae in cow's milk does cause disease. She believed this because other brucellae researchers throughout the world were reporting conclusions that supported her conviction.

She endured Dr. Smith's opposition, and that of the dairy industry, without animosity. Alice, the gentle microbe hunter, waged her battle temperately by plodding through stacks of tedious writings and ferreting out anything in literature about brucellae. She continued to work with cultures, searching always for the connection between diseased cows and undulant fever.

A mystery Alice was unable to solve until years later was related to Dr. Smith's change of stance about the danger of bovine brucella. She knew he had been researching cattle brucellosis for some time before 1918, the year Alice had published her paper. During that time he urged caution regarding the brucella microbe. Why would he reverse his position on the dangers of this microbe? We will soon learn that the greatest among us, even scientists, have weaknesses.

Chapter 13

Surrender – Never

*... "But once I had set out, I was
already far on my way."*
– Colette

We've skipped ahead in Alice's life to see how her "neurasthenia" dissolved. Now let's return to 1925. We find Alice continuing another fighting engagement.

Dr. William H. Welch, 75 years old at the time he entered the "Smith-Evans" controversy, had been chairman, since 1884, of the department of pathology at Johns Hopkins University Medical School. His was a distinguished career, and even though he officially retired from the Medical School, at this time he held the position of Dean of the School of Hygiene and Public Health of John Hopkins University. Dr. Hans Zinsser, Harvard bacteriologist and researcher, wrote that Theobald Smith and William Welch were "the two greatest individual influences that helped to hold the younger men working in the medical laboratories steadfast in the faith of worthiness of honest effort."

So here is Alice, afflicted with chronic undulant fever, yet reporting to work precisely on time, elevated temperature or not, and realizing that a top level medical officer, Smith, was bent on having her professional scalp!

On the spring day Dr. Welch walked into her life, Washington, D.C.'s cherry trees were bursting, pink and white, with spring blossoms. He stepped from the warm breezes and sunshine into the Hygienic Laboratory and as an advisory board member of this building, he had every reason to visit Alice's section.

Dr. Welch went to Dr. McCoy's office first. Looking back on it, Alice said she imagined that the two men must have discussed the controversy Theobald Smith had started. Alice felt sure that Smith had confided his doubts to McCoy concerning her work. She felt confident of McCoy's loyalty and scientific objectiveness, yet she wondered how he had told Dr. Welch of his trust in her "competence and integrity." How much would that mean to Dr. Welch?

In a short time, the two doctors sauntered into Alice's workspace. All was courtesy and shoptalk until just before the men turned to leave.

"I wish you and Dr. Smith would compose your differences in regard to brucellae," Dr. Welch said, his face earnest.

Alice, her inner self in turmoil, looked away and did not reply. There was everything to say. Yet no reply would make a grain of difference. She knew she could not change Dr. Smith's position.

Shortly afterward, The American Society of Tropical Medicine asked her to give a speech about where, in the

112

United States, brucellae was being reported. While she prepared her talk, Alice speculated about what might happen when she again made her point that this microbe flourished in the United States.

On the appointed day, nonetheless, she went ahead, and the audience members, in the discussion that followed her talk, made positive, kindly remarks. Dr. Welch stood up and ended the exchange of views.

"I cannot believe," he said, "that cow's milk might be the source of human infection."

Alice had to wonder no more. Dr. Welch, one of the medical greats, was in camp with Dr. Smith.

Dr. Welch concluded the meeting, then moved over to where Alice sat. Seating himself beside her, he again enjoined her to make up with Dr. Smith.

Alice lowered her eyes. She heartily wished she could respond. The evidence she had accumulated from her own experiments, added to supporting data that were coming from researchers in other countries, was giving her strength to persevere. Truth will out, be patient, the scientist in her whispered. But the human side shouted, perhaps, if you live long enough! She listened to the scientist hoping that silence would prove to be a mighty weapon.

****

Alice nodded at Dr. Welch's polite leave-taking. Now alone, rigid with indignation, she sat unseeing as members

113

chatted in small groups. She rose and slipped on her gloves, smoothing the wrinkles from each finger. She felt drowned in powerlessness.

With her face composed but shaking with suppressed emotions, Alice went home. She lay that night and pondered on what might happen to bring the conflict to a conclusion – and when.

Dr. Ludwig Hektoen helped move matters. He had been a friend to Alice in 1918, when Alice first announced her theory. Dr. Hektoen had been, at that time, editor of the Journal of Infectious Diseases and had promptly published Alice's reports. They became good friends in the intervening years. The doctor now directed medical sciences for the National Research Council. The job did not fill his time. Learning this, Dr. McCoy offered his colleague some vacant space in the Hygienic Laboratory.

For this reason, Dr. Hektoen entered her work domain. He set up a desk and workbench in Alice's laboratory, which had grown to encompass one entire end of the second floor. Most days he spent "a few" hours there. One afternoon, he and Alice happened to be working within speaking distance of each other.

Without taking his eye from the microscope, Dr. Hektoen said offhandedly, "I see that you and Dr. Smith are coming to a clash."

"Ludwig, I know nothing of this," Alice replied. "Tell me more, please."

She paused in her work, frowning. Here it is, she thought. The "expected unpleasantness."

"Well," he said, without his usual quick, sweet smile, "Theobald has been invited to take chairmanship of the Committee on Infectious Abortion of the National Research

Council. And you are going to be asked to be a committee member!"

Alice was stunned. A dozen thoughts raced in her head, stumbling over each other.

Dr. Hektoen went on. "Theobald declined the position by telegram. Then he followed it with a letter of explanation."

Remembering how long the conflict had gone on, Alice had a pretty good idea what his words would be. Ludwig told her briefly what was in the letter. The next day, he brought a copy. Alice sat down and read it slowly.

Generally, Dr. Smith said that he was studying some cultures of the "so-called Malta fever". One, or more, he said, was of the type Miss Evans had charged to the cow. He disagreed that any of the organisms were identical and he concluded that he would be in opposition to another committee member, (Alice, of course), and that his results would not be ready for publication for some months.

Alice, ever the objective writer, said many years later, that there was an excuse for Dr. Smith's "confusion". In 1914, she wrote, B. abortus was accepted as the cause of abortion in sows (porcine). This was the official name until 1928. Later, a new cultural technique was devised to tell the difference between bovine (cow) and porcine (pig) strains of brucella. Tests bacteriologists used until 1928 did not distinguish between the two strains.

Continuing the explanation, Alice reminds us that both she and Dr. Smith had puzzled over the Baltimore brucella strain. She emphasizes that with the knowledge available to scientists *at the time* she classified it properly as B. abortus (or Br. abortus). Dr. Smith compared this Baltimore strain with some he had from animals infected experimentally. He saw a difference in pathology. Seeking further, investigation of the Baltimore patient showed that he was a laboratory assistant and had contact with porcine tissues from a slaughter house. The strain later was classified as B. suis, or (Br. suis) thanks to the new standard of comparison. So they were both correct, using criteria available then.

At first, using the early agglutinin-absorption test, Alice identified the strain B. abortus. She wished that Dr. Smith could have studied these particular "Carpenter Cultures"; surely then he would realize their impact.

Alice had refused to be lured into a verbal battle when Dr. Smith first began disputing her research findings. Should she now go to her friends and colleagues within the laboratory? Should she ask for their support and then confront Dr. Smith with her experimental proof? Could she work harder and longer to perhaps come up with evidence that might persuade Dr. Smith to be more objective? How could she convince him that his question, "If undulant fever is transmittable, why aren't there more reported cases?" was tragically comic. There were few reported cases because most medical doctors lacked insight and knowledge about brucella, and were not interested in learning. Alice, a woman having no medical degree, insulted the medical profession with her declaration.

When Alice learned that Dr. Smith had openly expressed his lack of trust in her abilities to the National Research Council, anger made a decision easy. She would act on her own behalf.

Following the rules of her workplace, Alice went to Dr. McCoy.

"I appreciate your predicament, Alice, but I don't know of anything you can do with dignity," he said. "Truth will

116

prevail."

Alice set her teeth. How much longer must she wait for the truth! Breaking her long silence she said, "A man of Dr. Smith's stature could delay recognition of the truth for years," and turned away from Dr. McCoy. A wave of bitterness washed over her.

Desolation did not last. Alice pondered her predicament and rethought her perception of Dr. Welch as a henchman of Dr. Smith. Maybe Welch would be more fair-minded if she appealed personally to him.

Finally, she came up with the idea to draft a letter to Dr. Welch, asking him to intercede. She wrote, (in part), reminding Welch that he had asked her to resolve differences with Dr. Smith:

"It has been reported to me from another that Dr. Smith is strongly opposed to the idea that cattle may be the source of undulant fever in man. I am not personally acquainted with Dr. Smith and cannot very well address him on the subject, but since you seem to be in touch with his work I am writing this letter in order that if you see fit you may communicate with him when the opportunity comes.

It seems to me that Dr. Smith could not take the point of view that the so-called "Bacillus abortus" is non-pathogenic for man if he knew the evidence that has accumulated in the last few years in Italy and South Africa, as well as in this country."

Alice showed the letter to her chief, and he approved. "But don't expect a reply," McCoy cautioned. "Dr. Welch has a reputation for not writing letters."

Alice slid the envelope into the mail drop, her hopes less than high.

Chapter 14

Press on Regardless

"It may take patience, very hard work, a real struggle, and a long time, but it can be done. That much faith is a prerequisite of any undertaking..."
- Margo Jones

Forty-eight hours later came a letter from Dr. Welch. Alice could hardly believe her luck. Whether bad or good, she saw it was in the doctor's handwriting.

He wrote: "I am very much interested in your letter. I am taking the liberty of sending it to Theobald Smith. I think so highly of the both of you that if I can be the means of bringing about a rapport between you and him in this important study, I shall be gratified... If not too much trouble can you give me the references for the South Africa cases?"

Alice hastened to pull together a list taken from British and South African medical journals. In all, the publications documented 35 cases of human brucellosis caused by cows. She posted the articles by return mail.

Alice steeled herself for the unknown. A week passed, and Dr. Smith's reply arrived. Scanning it anxiously, Alice read: "Dr. Welch has kindly forwarded your letter bearing the relationship between **B. abortus and M. melitensis**. Thus far I have not published anything and I did not know that my private talks had any publicity."

Alice could well have sniffed and reminded him of the public remarks he had made about her work, whenever he had the chance. She went on to read: "On the whole, I think the accuracy of your work does not come in question as far as it has gone. Nor do I think it would suffer if you suspended judgment until the unknown factors responsible for or contributing to the incidence of human cases have been brought to light."

Dr. Smith might as well have written to the lady in the moon. Alice could not suspend judgment in so serious a matter. Every day lost in proving her point, she believed, meant people, especially children, became infected with undulant fever.

Now that she had been introduced to the eminent Dr. Smith, Alice pressed on with brucella research. Dr. Smith had a mind-change and busily spent the next six months reorganizing the National Research Council (A division of the Federal Departments of Biology and Agriculture). Surprisingly, Alice got an invitation to become a member of this Council! We wonder if she found any humor in the situation. Certainly, the easiest action would have been to refuse, thereby eliminating any possible confrontation.

Smith did have the power to make her life miserable.

Undaunted, Alice accepted the position in writing, and went to the meetings for six years, "without memorable incident", she said. Smith pulled in his horns, even as he clung to the position that raw milk was no danger to humans. Maybe he just could not admit his mistake, knowing that the adversary he himself had created was indeed correct. As time passed, he softened, and seemed to accept Alice as a scientist of integrity. Perhaps he began to take note of the increasing number of women medical officers in the experimental unit of the Public Health Service. In 1927, several of the Hygienic Laboratory personnel were women, highly educated and devoted to their careers. Times were changing.

That same year, a picture appeared in an eastern newspaper showing Alice and her associate, Dr. Elizabeth Verder. It is a laboratory setting, and in it Alice wears her usual immaculate, white starched uniform. She is 46 years old. Her brown hair has lightened and is cut with style; there is a small beginning of a double chin. The caption beneath reveals that Dr. Alice Evans (she has been given an honorary title by her colleagues) is the most famous of the N.I.H. scientists. She carries on her work, it says, in spite of poor health due to undulant fever.

It is doubtful if Alice saw herself as famous. True, she would be, next year, the first woman president of the Society of American Bacteriologists. (Her professional colleagues, encouraged by Dr. McCoy, at last acknowledged her rising fame, as more and more cases of undulant fever were diagnosed.)

She believed in herself, yes, as a scientist and a professional woman. It probably did not occur to her to

120

emulate masculine behavior in order to succeed as she struggled in a man's world. Erect of carriage, impeccably dressed, always poised, Alice would be considered today a well adjusted, successful person. In 1927 she was a rarity.

Alice's relationship with Dr. Elizabeth Verder brought out a shadowy side of Alice. According to a woman colleague, (a microbiologist with a Ph.D.) Alice was assigned "Beth" as an associate. In time it became evident that there was less than perfect cooperation between them. Beth had studied at the prestigious University of Chicago; earned her doctor's degree there. Others noticed she had excellent organizational skills, but seemed to be a perfectionist. Beth did not hesitate to point out where she thought Alice should do differently. This apparently brought on a certain amount of testiness in Alice.

One evening a mutual friend and colleague gave a dinner party at her home for the area's outstanding medical women. Alice, of course, was invited, Beth was not. To her embarrassment, the hostess received a scathing letter from Alice. Evidently, whatever resentful feelings Alice had toward young Beth, loyalty for her as a co-worker superseded them.

A possible explanation for Alice's reaction could be the wretched state of her health at this time, or it might have been fatigue or jealousy. Dealing with Theobald Smith on a more or less distant plane, though stressful, was different from the daily working problems one has with an associate. It might have stemmed from envy of one who had the degree Alice would have liked earlier in her career, from her dreamed-of university. (Although, much later, she downplayed her term of study there as of little use to her.)

Meanwhile, Alice's work relationship deepened with

Hans Zinsser. He was still researching at Harvard Medical School in the Department of Bacteriology and Immunology. Alice first mentioned this doctor, who would become a revered colleague, in her memoirs of the 1924 era, when she quoted Zinsser as saying the Drs. Welsh and Smith were the "two greatest influences...to younger men." Perhaps by now, Alice wondered if the women workers felt the same loyalty.

A correspondence began between Alice and Hans in June of 1927. He wrote asking for her cooperation in sending certain germ strains to an assistant while he, Zinsser, spent the rest of the summer in France. One sentence "...since I regard any serious contention you may formulate as well worth following up, however much I may be inclined to disagree..." sets the tone. Zinsser viewed Alice's reputation as worthy, at the same time dissenting with her position on some issues. During this time, undulant fever again attacked Alice. She read many letters from Hans in her bed in the United States Public Health Service Hospital, #82, at Tanner's Creek, Norfolk, Virginia. Zinsser asked for assistance regarding a student who wished to study "abortus infections" and the doctor posed several complicated questions. He apologized twice for the "deluge of letters" and wrote: "You are the authority, namely, on the abortus infections in man."

She was still in the hospital when she received a short letter in December, 1927. Hans said he was considering the use of an encephalitis problem as the subject of a Mellon Lecture planned for springtime. He asked permission to include Alice's views on mutation. He wrote: "I should not like to omit mentioning any work of yours..." continuing, "Yet there might be...things that you (are) not ready to talk about."

Poor Alice, still sick and in a different hospital (Johns Hopkins) revived sufficiently to reply: "...I would really prefer that you would not mention my virus in your Mellon Lecture – not because I object to your statement... but because you state, later on, that the transition (I object to the term 'mutation' for these changes,) from bacteria form to filterable virus remains to be proven, or in other words, you do not believe the origin of the Dishman virus could be as I have stated.

"After my paper describing how I obtained the Dishman virus has been published, of course I can make no objection to how anyone regards it, but it would be an injustice to have the announcement of my method of obtaining this virus made under such inauspicious circumstances as your lecture. I shall be very glad to receive a copy of your lecture."

Her words left little doubt about her feelings. Alice had labored long on this project, and considered it too important to be revealed in a lowly lecture, no matter how distinguished the speaker. Hans fired back a humble reply, but would not budge. "...I cannot accept the transformation..."

A word of explanation: The term "virus", at that time included all infectious pathogens. Apparently, Alice was arguing that the "Dishman virus" came about as the result of a transformation in a bacterium. This theory about the origin of viruses was popular in the days before the electron microscope. If this were the case, Alice was wrong and Zinsser was correct. We now know viruses do not originate from transformed bacteria.

During this illness, as in her previous episodes, Dr. McCoy came to her hospital room often, bringing news and stories of the laboratory; he buoyed up her spirits and made her feel like a beloved family member. Deftly, he juggled figures around in such a way as to keep her on the payroll after her sick leave stopped. This was a continuation of his striking loyalty to Alice, for it had been McCoy who urged her to join professional organizations and volunteer for positions of responsibility within them. It was he who gave quick permission for newspaper and magazine publicity about her (and others, too, within the Institute).

Hans Zinsser's last correspondence, for the time being, was dated October, 1928, and addressed to the Hygienic Laboratory. Alice was back on the job. Dr. Zinsser said he hoped to continue to discuss and correspond with her "...because with all that we have found out, we have not gone much farther in elucidating the encephalitis problem."

The same year, 1928, Smith published a paper, saying briefly, "if it were assumed that B. abortus produces a diseased condition in man", it would create a crucial, expensive situation within the dairy industry. He urged more research on brucella be undertaken. Alice tried to stem her frustration. She realized that short-sightedness can be a weakness even in such notable scientists as Koch and Smith. But recognizing the problem didn't make it go away. Alice waited, prayed and kept on working.

She knew that back in 1925 "...five cases of human brucellosis not traceable to goats had been recognized in the United States...and Dr. L.E.W. Bevan reported to the Royal Society of Medicine in London, that 35 cases of brucellosis had been diagnosed in Southern Rhodesia in persons who could not have received infection from goats."

Bevan had read Alice's reports about the relationship between B. abortus and M. melitensis four years earlier and was quoted as saying he began to "think furiously." Bevan, a veterinarian, got permission to peruse hospital records and discovered that a lot of "obscure" illnesses originated in rural areas where there was no contact with goats. Eventually a feverish patient showed up who lived in an area where Bevan had seen cattle with infections. Bevan persuaded the doctor to allow him to draw a sample of the patient's blood. What he found made his own blood heat up. The test "…gave a positive agglutination reaction with the standard suspension of <u>B. abortus</u>…" Bevan reported the case in the January, 1922, issue of <u>Transactions of the Royal Society of Tropical Medicine and Hygiene.</u>

****

We can see, then, why Alice said, "In 1925 an awareness of human brucellosis of bovine origin began to develop…" In the United States, Dr. Carpenter in the east and Dr. Meyer on the west coast were diligently researching and speaking out, urging medical doctors to learn about undulant fever. By the end of this year, a total of 12 "widely scattered cases were recognized" and the causal organism binding them together was <u>B. abortus</u>, with evidence heavily weighted toward cows as the source of infection.

A dozen cases aren't many, but to Alice it must have seemed like the beginning of a beautiful dream. Other researchers were finding and reporting undulant fever cases; the rising curve was steady and peaked in 1947 at 6,321 cases.

"Obviously," she said, "the rapid increase in the number of reported cases was due largely, if not entirely, to the growing awareness of the disease. The decline in the number of reported cases following the peak in 1947 may be attributed partly to the increased usage of pasteurized milk and other dairy products; the chief factor was the gradual elimination of disease from cattle."

The dairy industry relived the tuberculosis trauma in 1934, when a program of brucellosis eradication began on both the state and federal level. Animals reacting positive to a test for infection were slaughtered and the owner was paid by the government for the animal. A better method, vaccination of calves, was introduced about 1940. By the next year, 1941, the incidence of infected cattle went down to 2.4% from the high of 11.5% indicated by the first series of tests.

Today state animal health laboratories use several tests for finding brucellosis infections. Michigan uses two tests - tube agglutination and plate agglutination - which are run from blood samples.

We return to 1928. While Dr. Smith maintained his doubts, Alice continued to find and study reports of human brucellosis cases of the bovine type, which were being diagnosed from many countries abroad. Progress toward recognition of undulant fever was being made. But how fast, how far would these researches and reports go to prove her theory?

"The floodgates were open... regarding hundreds of cases of confirmed undulant fever," Sir Dalrymple-Champneys of Great Britain stated. Alice would meet him in London four years hence. But where would those research waters take the study? How many years behind times would the United States scientists be before admitting to their error?

Chapter 15

Sara and Paul Make An Impact

"The fat was in the fire."
- Alice Evans

Between her assigned work in the laboratory and "her special project" Alice pushed herself to the limit. It was 1929, the year of the tragic stock market breakdown, the beginning of our country's most terrible economic depression. Alice was one of the rare fortunates, for it did not affect her job. Thankful, she remained secure because of the overwhelming need for public assistance. Then, more than in any previous era, our government recognized hunger and disease epidemics and acted immediately.

Taking time off only when the chronic fever and chills overpowered her, Alice toiled long tedious hours. Encephalitis, the dreaded sleeping sickness, partially occupied her professional time.

Meningitis strains that Alice worked with during World War I which gave victims red splotches, neck rigidity and insomnia were but a few of many different kinds. Alice and Sara and their co-workers studied these microbes. They found that the illness could be brought on, apparently, by almost any other germ! It is spread by droplets from the nose and mouth, and the infection damages the meninges, the membranes that shield the spinal column and brain.

Dr. Sara Elizabeth Branham, dazzling in her intellect and accomplishments, had joined the family of the Hygienic Laboratory the previous year. Dr. McCoy had recruited her to work on the mystery of meningitis, a study that excited Sara's imagination and wooed her away from an associate's position at the School of Medicine at the University of Rochester. She went on to earn a medical doctor's degree at the University of Chicago, while employed in Washington. McCoy's paternal hand, supporting, cultivating, is evident here and Sara Branham thrived. She became a diplomate in both the National Board of Medical Examiners and the American Board of Pathology. She quickly evolved into a world-class expert on meningitis and by 1965 had published more than 70 research papers in Bacteriology and Immunology.

Shapely Sara, with her regular features, silky dark blonde curly hair and Georgia accent seemed out-of-place when she first picked up her tools at the Hygienic Laboratory. She looked as if she should be back in the fundamentally religious little town of Oxford, in the role of proper wife and mother. A gracious, warm-hearted woman, she found that being a member of McCoy's laboratory family was as fulfilling as life could be.

This was McCoy's directive to Sara Branham: Find a cure for the coffee-bean-shaped meningitis microbe which was overwhelming patients' bloodstreams with infection, often killing them within hours.

First, Branham thought she had to discover why horse serum, which had been fairly successful earlier, had no effect on the present epidemic of meningitis. She threw herself into information gathering and accumulated the largest pile of data on meningitis in the world. Sara found that sulfonamide emerged while a German chemist, Gerhard Domask, was searching for a dye that would set better in woolens. Sulfur is a non-metallic chemical element, light yellow in color. The word, sulfonamide, would soon come to specify the sulfur drugs that could be used for certain bacterial infections.

One day Dr. Sanford Rosenthal, a pharmacologist, poked his head in Sara's work-station. As he stood chatting, a thought came to him.

"How about trying sulfanilamide?" he asked. "Maybe in association with various new sera you've been studying."

Sara's superb research instinct snapped to attention. The most electrifying week of her life began as she set up experiments with the new coal tar synthetic. She prepared four cages of mice and hurried to work each morning to study them. Within days the results pointed at a simple cure. With mounting excitement she saw that the horse serum and sulfanilamide together protected the meningitis-injected mice even though they harbored 100,000 times the amount needed to kill them! Sara checked and rechecked. The results remained consistent and she wasted no time arranging for a final test. If this experiment were successful, disease control would claim a major discovery!

Sara arranged for meningitis-infected charity patients

in the shabby Gallinger Hospital to receive her antidote. Within forty-eight hours miraculous - and consistent - recoveries occurred. The swift deaths of about 25% of meningitis patients no longer would be expected. Most patients injected with Sara Branham's serum and drug combination could, within minutes, sit up in bed. After a day or two of observation, they were well enough to walk out of the hospital. What an achievement!

Alice and Sara were becoming close friends; we wonder how Alice responded inwardly to "Sally's" quick success. We know Alice as one with a generous spirit. Yet her own struggle for recognition had been so painful and long in coming Alice must have wished she could have shared, during those early years, a portion of Sara's good fortune.

We sense that Alice truly shared the joy and pride of achievement with this woman who must have been like a sister to her. Surely it strengthened Alice's resolve to stay with the brucella battle to the end, even though she had to put it aside in favor of other assignments.

She did not, however, let go of it. Keeping abreast of current statistics, she noted that in Ohio and Iowa, by 1930, 465 cases of human brucellosis came to light. The Ohio sources of the infection apparently originated in cow's milk. The Iowa diseases came from patients handling infected animals, carcasses or tissues. There were more of the porcine (sow) type than bovine (cow), in this midwestern state.

Still, leading bacteriologists in the dairy industry repeated the basic question: "If there were know cases of cattle being infected with brucellosis in communities all over the country, why weren't more humans catching the disease?"

Alice knew the answer. People did catch undulant fever

130

and doctors were not recognizing it. She said it in 1917, but no one believed her. The medical profession should have paid attention to the little lady who now wore her gray-streaked brown hair cut very short and sported knee-length fashionable dresses. She was the heroine of Bang and Bruce microbes' research and was doing outstanding work on streptococci.

Decades later, when an historian at the National Institutes of Health asked Alice to write her memoirs, she arranged her thoughts, went to her desk and began. It was her 82nd year. She had had time to reflect on the reasons for her long years of struggle.

In Chapter 9 she wrote: "I am sorry this chapter may be painful to friends of one of the most eminent bacteriologists. Among great scientists Theobald Smith is not alone, however, in his resistance to a new scientific idea."

Summarizing what Bernard Barber said in his lecture to the American Association for the Advancement of Science, she wrote: "Scientists are probably the most objective of researchers. Unfortunately, they can be influenced by their social system."

She continued by giving illustrations from Barber citing history in which famous scientists resisted ideas from a lesser investigator. Alice was saying, "My circumstances, exactly!"

Then she finished the chapter by writing, "I was a newcomer in the field where he [Dr. Theobald Smith] was regarded as an authority...and he was not accustomed to considering a scientific idea proposed by a woman." But making an issue out of sex discrimination in 1929, only nine years after women won the vote, would have been nothing more than a cry in the wind.

The wrangling dragged on between the dairymen who produced certified raw milk and those who worried about safe milk. Dairymen had readily made their herds available for tuberculosis inspection and felt they were being reasonable in protesting the added expense of pasteurization. They advertised that their cows were "certified" free of tuberculosis. Their milk was clean, they said, and the stories about undulant fever surely were exaggerations.

Alice, in a late memorandum to her Memoirs said:

"...I did not try to follow it, for by that time I was removed from direct contact with dairy problems, and my mind was occupied with other matters. But occasionally I was reminded of the strife."

The Ladies' Home Journal of September, 1929, published an article entitled 'Before You Drink A Glass of Milk', by Paul de Kruif. In its preparation he had interviewed me two or three times. The article, advocating pasteurization of all milk, was widely read. It inflamed the controversy."

Paul de Kruif had become a best-seller historian/author of medical adventure and discovery. Nine years younger than Alice, he earned a doctor's degree in bacteriology from the University of Michigan, and soon after joined the army of World War I. During the war he produced a serum which prevented gas gangrene in injuries. Afterward he went back to more bacteriological research at the University of Michigan and the Rockefeller Institute.

In 1922, his book, Our Medicine Men appeared in bookstores. In it de Kruif openly criticized current medical practices. Naturally, it offended some doctors and enraged others in the highly esteemed profession. It brought de Kruif to the attention of Sinclair Lewis with whom he collaborated on the classic novel, <u>Arrowsmith</u>. By the time de Kruif interviewed Alice he had already become popular with his 1926 book, <u>The Microbe Hunters,</u> in which he dramatized the struggles of early men who initiated and developed the science of bacteriology.

An article in the February, 1930, issue of <u>Good Housekeeping</u> refuted de Kruif's views. It was entitled "Undulant Fever: What It Is and How It Concerns You", by Frederic Damrau, M.D. and approved by Dr. Walter H. Eddy, Director of Good Housekeeping Bureau of Foods, Sanitation and Health. Dr. Damrau emphasized the rarity of recognized cases of undulant fever and he quoted the Secretary of the American Association of Medical Milk Commissions, who said that "great weight must be given to the fact that there has never been a case of undulant fever in a child proved to be due to the use of certified milk." He advised that since "certified milk is guaranteed to have so low a germ content...pasteurization would be superfluous."

Now, Alice wrote,

"The fat was in the fire. Reverberations reached me through relatives who were affected from various points of involvement. My brother, Morgan, attending a meeting in Columbus, Ohio, of the state's agricultural leaders, overheard a table conversation among a group unaware he was my brother. One of them said that Paul de Kruif was paid $20,000 for writing his recent article. This remark was a reflection of the belief, common among dairymen, that the manufacturers of pasteurizing equipment were financing the crusade against raw milk.

I corresponded with only three persons involved in the controversy... Coming from the grass roots, they reveal the fever of the dispute.

There was correspondence with the Milk and Food Inspector of Everett, Washington, who happened to be my cousin. For several reasons, partly on account of poor health [even here Alice plays down her chronic fever bouts] also because I did not want to become an active participant in the controversy, I did not ask the Hygienic Laboratory to send me to the convention of dairy officials of the Pacific Northwest to which he invited me.

A few months after the women's journals published articles for and against pasteurization of certified milk, I received a letter from a milk dealer of Tulsa, Oklahoma, whose firm was carrying on a 'campaign to teach the people on Tulsa the health value of pasteurized milk.' Then I received another letter from Tulsa, from the wife of a relative whose family owned a dairy farm producing certified milk on the outskirts of the city. A leader of the opposition, she wrote hoping I would confirm the opinion of Dr. Damrau, published in Good Housekeeping. Her letter was delivered to me as I was leaving home to catch a train that took me to the boat on which I sailed to Europe. I answered the letter in handwriting on the boat and mailed it from Scotland...I told her essentially what I had written to her opponent. She has not forgiven me."

Alice continued, saying that in 1932, Paul de Kruif discussed the same controversy. In quoting from his book, Men Against Death she wrote,"...with what whispers (very portentous) the affair was spoken of in agricultural and dairy circles. It was considered too dangerous to talk about, let alone publish broadcast..."

So much had happened this year of 1929. Alice again

lay in John Hopkins Hospital in Baltimore, enduring another siege of undulant fever. She had plenty of time to reflect on her struggle to be heard, the dispute with Theobald Smith, and her good fortune in having Dr. Carpenter to do the leg work in proving the connection between infected cows and brucellosis. Now there was the live-wire Dr. Walter Simpson, carrying on in Ohio what Carpenter started in New York. Life could have been sweeter only if, by a miracle, her chronic pain and hospitalization were to vanish. Dr. Smith's objections to her theory had begun to wane. He was 70 years old, and probably in poor health, for he died five years later. Reports arrived at the Institute from all the states, and all over the world, citing cases of human brucellosis contracted from cows. Smith was dean of our country's medical men, true, but he seemed unable to shrug off the dairy industry's pressure to oppose costly pasteurization. Nineteen-twenty-nine was the year Smith published his last "lingering doubts" about the brucella microbe being connected to "Malta fever."

How could Alice, the shy nobody, do more than she'd already done?

What had sustained Alice in her purpose and goals through the years of rejection and criticism?

Moral courage held her steadfastly to her course, courage derived from strong family values, and her Welsh heritage of believing in one's own self-worth. Alice was blessed with superior intelligence, and in the tradition of Welsh perseverance and high principles, ingrained from both home and church training, she met her world with stout defenses. And she was warmly human, this woman who had been described in her youth as a Welsh girl, with a quick, humorous glance and a tentative, restrained giggle.

Yes, Alice did not take herself too seriously.

Bacteriology, on the other hand, was a different glove. A journalist, delineating Alice's life observed..." No activity seems to be as interesting to her as her work."

The writer did not address Alice's personal life in the article. Had she done so, she could have told about Alice's intense love of family, about Alice remaining unmarried but in close contact with her immediate kinfolk and a multitude of cousins everywhere in this country and in Wales.

Morgan's children were especially precious to Alice. Her brother had settled into a position as a plant breeder in Ohio with the Federal Department of Agriculture. He and his wife, Zoe, had three children, Anna, Marvin and Sarah, between 1918 and 1925. During these years Morgan managed to earn a Master of Science degree at George Washington University.

Sarah, the youngest, remembers a fashionably dressed Aunt Alice arriving in Cleveland by train, in the summertime, when the family would pick her up and Morgan would drive his black car to their home in North Ridgeville, Ohio. When he moved his family to Wooster, Ohio, Sarah recalls that her aunt sometimes visited several weeks at a time.

Regarding her own childhood, Sarah wrote that her Aunt Alice "...enjoyed working in the garden and helping with the cooking. She always went to [the Congregational] church with us...although she did have a brief membership with the Unitarians..."

Sarah has early memories of Alice as an honored guest at Christmas time, too." I can remember several pretty outfits Aunt Alice gave me as gifts," she said.

Alice's family tree grew with the marriages of her nieces and nephew and their children. Later Sarah recollected, "After I was married and had a family, Aunt Alice came and visited us." We can picture Alice, wearing her favorite color, navy blue, in a dress whose hem line was much higher off the ground than in her younger days; matching sailor hat on her close-cut hairdo, and a carefully selected necklace or brooch.

****

In this pivotal year of solid progress, 1929, Alice had much upon which to ruminate as she learned to pace herself in the hospital. At times when the fever and pain diminished, she would slide out of bed and walk about her room and the halls, returning when her tormented knee joints cried for relief. Resting, she must have contemplated Dr. Carpenter's role in her career. The "horse doctor" from Ithaca, New York, who correctly diagnosed the two college students as having undulant fever, had made known his gratitude to her; we can only wonder why, in her memoirs, she awarded him with only six sentences for his work in proving her premise, and nothing at all about his forceful exposé of infected "certified milk" in Ithaca, New York.

She often thought back to Dr. Walter Simpson and his energetic presence in the Midwest. Tall, vigorous Dr. Simpson, his heavy hair parted neatly on the side, had launched a crusade in his job as pathology chief in the Miami Valley Hospital in Dayton, Ohio. This Scottish - American doctor set out to prove Alice Evans correct and to compel passage of a state law requiring pasteurization of all milk. Wrote de Kruif, in an eloquent description of Simpson, the doctor was ..."almost as much an undulant fever Sherlock Holmes as is Carpenter..."

Dr. Simpson urged his staff to aggressively search for cases of undulant fever, especially those which might be undiagnosed. Alice would be delighted the next year, 1930, to learn that the man who became "her good friend" and his brucellosis division had uncovered more than 70 cases of the disease in the local area! A third of the diagnoses they arrived at without the help of the laboratory until after they located the patients! What a change from ten years earlier, when Alice had trouble convincing doctors she was finding brucella microbes in blood samples they sent her.

Simpson, impatient that people should suffer, when prevention was as near as vats of milk heated to 145 degrees Fahrenheit, spared no energy in himself or his workers. He confirmed that in all of the instances, infection came from cow's milk. In five patients, Br. abortus turned up in a culture, and the laboratory was able to bring up an identical strain from the milk the patients had been drinking. Simpson was to discover, as he dashed about Dayton brucella - searching, that two doctors in Denmark had found 500 patients with Br. abortus infections! This happened during a 20 month period. How could there be any doubt now?

Walter Simpson, ever the gentleman, made it known he owed Alice Evans a debt for placing him on the highway to eradicating undulant fever. She, in turn, acknowledged Dr. Simpson in her memoirs, "Simpson made significant contributions to a wider understanding of the chronic phase of the disease in his chapter of brucellosis in the several revised editions of Tice's Practice of Medicine". She recorded also Dr. Hardy's extensive work on brucellosis in Iowa, and called both men "pioneers."

138

Chapter 16

Looking "Over the Top"

> *"Medical research workers are very much like children piling a ladder of boxes against a garden wall. When we have had a sufficient number of contributions to knowledge we can see over the top."*
>
> - Dr. Sara Branham

"The infection is transmitted from animals to humans." The textbook, <u>Current Medical Diagnosis and Treatment</u>, 1991 edition, begins the second paragraph about brucellosis with this statement.

In plain, straight forward language it describes a tangle of mismanaged medical history. Alice's paramount avenue to the truth, her publications, placed her under attack from esteemed, notable men. She suffered the misery of infection with <u>Br. melitensis</u>, the goat strain of brucellosis. At its worst, this germ clusters on the brains of its victims and sends them, eventually, to their death. At its best it causes severe and disabling pain. Alice, with a little smile, said, "It seems as if those bugs had a special animosity toward me since I made that discovery."

This should have been the prime time of her life. Yet nowhere in her story are there indications she ever considered surrendering. Alice clung to her investigations, collecting and verifying, always believing.

In time, all humanity would benefit by Alice's discovery, particularly people in the United States. Villages, counties, then states invoked pasteurization laws. Infection-free dairy products made a stunning contribution to public health as did preventative animal vaccines. If Alice had not hung on, believing in her research, publishing her findings, both human and animal suffering would have been prolonged.

Today, human brucellosis is treated by combinations of drugs. One union is doxycycline and rifampin or streptomycin (all three can be used); another is trimethroprim-sulfamethoxazol with rifampin or streptomycin, or both, given for 21 days.

Surprisingly, Europe has a lower incidence of bovine brucellosis that the United States. Taking this country's vast areas of cattle ranches into consideration, perhaps the statistic of 200 reported US. cases yearly is to be expected. What seems inexcusable is that knowledgeable estimates indicate that only about four percent of the cases are diagnosed! That means for each hundred slaughterhouse workers, livestock producers, farmers, butchers, and veterinarians, (plus those who consume unpasteurized milk products), who become ill from this bacteria, 96 of them are not treated for the disease.

In early April of 1991, the Associated Press carried two articles detailing the events before and after park rangers shot and killed three Yellowstone Park bison. It was an attempt, the story said, to discover if any of a herd of 25 bison had brucellosis.

Members of the Fund for Animals group, alarmed that a government official would be so uncaring or ignorant of a simple blood test for the disease, got a restraining order and the remaining buffaloes were spared. Katherine A. Meyer, attorney for this group, called the destruction illegal. Living tissue and blood samples, she said, can be used to detect brucellosis. Ms. Meyer won her case. Montana received so much adverse publicity that Governor Stan Stevens quickly signed a bill which stopped the sale of buffalo hunting licenses. The Associated Press reported that the story began in 1985 when the Montana Legislature allowed the sale of hunting licenses to shoot the buffalo which move north into Montana in winter searching for food. The reasoning behind the order was to protect Montana cattle herds from possible brucellosis-infected Yellowstone bison. During the first winter of 1988-89, after the disastrous Yellowstone fires, more than 500 bison were destroyed in Montana pastures.

Many of the killing scenes were recorded by television and newspaper photographers. People all over the country reacted. As a result, only 15 bison were killed in the two years following, until the April incident.

****

In her lifetime, Alice had rubbed elbows with numerous intriguing, famous individuals, but none was more fascinating than Paul de Kruif. A large, powerfully built man, with thinning hair, intense dark eyes and a small mustache, he made the air crackle with his presence in her hospital room that spring day in 1929. What an abundance of healthy good nature shone around him! How medically expert he was!

Alice let herself be charmed as she traveled back in time to recount the heartbreak and attainment of the past dozen years. When de Kruif left, she slid down and rested her head on the pillow. She was pleasantly exhausted. Smiling, she thought about the next interview and anticipated those moments with delight; they were probably her happiest times as she marked the dull passage of the days toward recovery from this long siege of undulant fever.

Within days she received the following excerpted letter, badly typed and hand-noted, from de Kruif's own typewriter.

"Dear Miss Evans:

I am head-over-heels into the story, and am having a noble time with it. It will certainly be a small antidote to the publicity stunt put out in the Washington papers last autumn, though surely nobody will be able to take offense at it. I have noted what you say about the reception of your work by medical men, and there again please don't worry...

Can you do just one more thing for me? You remember showing me a picture of you in what seemed to be a graduation costume the day Mrs. de Kruif and I visited you two weeks ago. (When was it taken approximately?) I wonder could you send it on right away. I shall take good care of it, and send it back intact. There's a chance, from the way my story is now shaping up, that the magazine will want to use it as well as the photos I already have.

I do hope you will soon be feeling entirely fit. It's been a great inspiration to me to have had the chance to tackle your story. Mrs. de Kruif joins me in the kindest regards and best wishes."

The widely read article, entitled "Before You Drink a Glass of Milk" came out in September, 1929, (but did not run Alice's Towanda graduation picture.) Pleased with public response, de Kruif used this article, along with other pieces he wrote, in his book, <u>Men Against Death</u>.

****

Gray wintertime hung about Washington like a damp coat, chilling bodies, depressing minds, especially those of the medical researchers working on the tragic disease, Parrot fever (psittacosis.) Although Alice did not work on the new project, Sally Branham did, so Alice was acutely aware of the activities which engaged her outstanding friend. With Charles Armstrong and George McCoy, the trio always seemed to be in a hurry, trotting from the laboratories to the lower levels and running back up again. Sally signed as foremost researcher and writer along with Armstrong and McCoy in the US. Public Health Report,

Bacillus psittacosis in Nocard, 1893. Failure to find it in the 1929-1930 epidemic in the United States.

They competed with time; four out of five afflicted persons in Europe had died, and in this country 75 cases were confirmed. Of these, 14 had died.

Doctors Armstrong and McCoy immediately took over two basement rooms in the old Hygienic Building. They bought garbage cans and fitted screens over the tops to be used as parrot cages. Into them went all kinds of parrots; healthy, feverish, nearly dead birds. No one was allowed into these smelly rooms except the doctors. McCoy thrust all protocol aside and substituted for the lab helper, Shorty, whom Armstrong said was the world's best "lab swipe." Shorty had contracted psittacosis and was becoming sicker each day at the Naval Hospital next door.

McCoy drudged at the menial job of caring for birds, experimenting with parts of the diseased dead ones, making sure he wiped his shoes carefully on the creosote-soaked mat outside. Eventually, they found that the germ passed from bird to bird and from bird to humans.

As Shorty's illness progressed, Armstrong and McCoy, and their assistants kept close watch on him. Shorty suffered an unbearable headache. He was feverish and his lungs filled with a sticky fluid. He coughed incessantly, became weaker. McCoy made a solution of fluids taken from Shorty and injected healthy parrots. The birds died.

So did various innocent owners who had sick pet parrots. Within a few weeks, the death count rose to 20 from the disease. Yet, folks generally thought little of it...those who were greatly attached to their pets paid scant attention. The newspaper Cal Bulletin in San Francisco, quoted the famous microbe chaser, Dr. Karl Meyer, saying he "[believes in the] theory that parrots carried death [germ] in East."

Suddenly, it hit home. Workers, from maintenance to medical doctors began falling ill with parrot fever. Dr. Armstrong was one of the ten victims to be taken to the Naval Hospital. This left Dr. McCoy and Sara burdened with the tragic puzzle. Shorty died. His colleagues rallied around, frightened and sad, and collected funds to pay his bills, wondering who would be next.

Desperate, McCoy called Dr. Spencer and sent him out to comb the eastern coast of the country. "Find recovered psittacosis persons," he ordered. "Pay them anything to give you some of their blood."

Away went Spenny, armed with needles, tubes and syringes. The first five people he located, gave him a big NO. He could not offer them enough money, they said. They had been through too much already. The sixth was a tiny old lady, who was pleased to help even though she was still frail and weak. Dr. Spencer took a goodly amount of her blood and hurried back to Washington. There he made a serum, quickly gave it to the hallucinating Dr. Armstrong and the afflicted lab workers. Within two hours, Dr. Armstrong said later, he floated away in a peaceful sleep, like a baby. The others recovered too, including Sadie Carlin, bacteriologist, who had worked with the psittacosis cultures. Sadie, Alice, Sara and others had shared the meningocci study, before and after the parrot fever tragedy.

McCoy was baffled. None of the 10 workers had been in the parrot room. Sadie had been in the den next door to the bird room. Alice's sterling friend, Dr. Ludvig Hoekten was ill, too, and he had only walked by the open door of

McCoy's autopsy room.

Dr. McCoy remained immune, for reasons still unknown. He ordered the evacuation of all workers and lab animals, except the parrot fever experimental birds, guinea pigs and mice (which he disposed of humanely). The big brick building on the hill was sealed – doors, windows and vents, and flooded with enough cyanide gas to kill an army.

When workers returned, all was sterile. The ten patients at the hospitals recovered. They had received the life-saving serum Spenny and technicians made from the nameless little old heroine. This illness still ranks as one of the most contagious diseases known.

Charles Armstrong, lightning fast, took the psittacosis work away from the Hygienic Lab. He and the watchman, Lanham, moved everything to an old empty building in Baltimore. Toiling there in isolation would be safer for everyone.

****

In 1930, the Hygienic Laboratory, with a staff of 133, became known as the National Institute of Health (N.I.H.). Alice had just passed what was to be the halfway mark in her life. This second life-portion began with a voyage to Europe. The trip thrilled Alice; in her <u>Memoirs</u> she devotes 14 pages to the description.

Two colleagues left Washington with her that summer day in 1930. One was Dr. Eloise Cram, a parasitologist, who was headed for a science congress in London. Dr. Cram was making remarkable contributions to the study of

146

veterinary parasitology in the Bureau of Animal Industry. Six years later she would transfer to take over as chief of the helminthological (study of worm-like parasites) section of the Division of Zoology. This was an even more remarkable event, for although this was the lowest management level at the National Institute of Health, Eloise was the only woman to reach it in the 1930's.

An attractive woman, her striking, outgoing personality charmed everyone. Unfailingly friendly and hard-working, her high intellect and skill elevated her to the presidency of the American Association of Parasitologists.

The prestigious directory, "American Men of Science," refused to recognize her promotion and listed her (Eloise's star was so bright they could not ignore her) as "with" the N.I.H. in the late 1930's.

Alice, Sara Branham and Ida Bengtson never attained "star status", meaning that they were not included in the annual "American Men of Science" list of one-thousand top scientists of the United States.

The other traveler on this trip was "Sally" Branham. Apparently this was Alice's pet name for her close friend, for she used it when describing their social experiences. Sara attended the First International Congress of Microbiology in Paris as a delegate from the United States.

They had no intention of going directly to these meetings. This was VACATION! Spirits high, Alice, Sarah and Eloise boarded the train for Montreal. They arrived a day early to sightsee.

Their ship was the *Duchess of Richmond*. It slipped away from the wharf the morning of June 27 on its first trip of the year on a charted northern route to the Atlantic Ocean. Earlier in the season, the steamship company used the southern route, around Newfoundland, to avoid icebergs.

The *Duchess* sailed past Quebec at sundown, on a fog-shrouded St. Lawrence River. When Alice and her friends awoke next morning, they discovered they weren't much closer to the Atlantic Ocean than the night before.

By the time they steamed slowly throughout the Gulf of St. Lawrence, the fog had thinned. Alice watched from the deck, warmly dressed, as they drew nearer to the coast of Labrador. She spied "patches of snow and ice" on the island.

That same afternoon, the weather having moderated, Alice sat on deck with nearly every other passenger on board. As they looked over the deck railing, out of the mist like a ghostly mountain, an enormous iceberg began to materialize. It seemed to be traveling straight at the ship on a crash course.

Alice wrote, "The chill of it was on our faces; the splendor of it was overwhelming, the threat of it was terrifying." It rushed at the ship; gleaming, greenish-opal, twin peaks separated by a deep, icy valley. "Everyone remained seated quietly, except for an occasional exclamation or gasp; a few wept. Hypnotized best describes my state of mind."

Desperately, the captain turned the huge rudders, and only 200 yards from the "dreadful, majestic object," the ship veered.

The crisis past, shaken passengers found their voices. Alice heard someone mention the *Titanic* tragedy of 18 years ago, when the colossal, brand-new luxury ship hit an iceberg, drowning hundreds of persons. Alice wrote that nothing at all had entered her mind during the emergency; she was "spellbound."

Southward through water-clinging clouds they went, changing course to skirt the southern side of Labrador and thus miss the icebergs. Passengers then saw the same scenery again as they made a U turn and proceeded on the northern route. The fog did rise; Alice counted almost two dozen icebergs, including the one which had "hypnotized" her!

Nine days after leaving Montreal, the *Duchess* docked at Greenock, Scotland. Alice, Sarah and Eloise disembarked and toured beautiful southern Scotland for a week "...after which we separated," Alice wrote, "each to visit a place of her especial interest. I went to France."

Alice belonged to several professional groups throughout her lifetime, one of them being the American Association of University Women. Now the membership was proving to be useful. During the weeks Alice and Sara Branham enjoyed the hospitality of France, they stayed at Reid Hall, the American Association of University Women's Paris Center. A comfortable accommodation, it was close to the Pasteur Institute where preparations for the First International Congress of Microbiology hummed along. She arrived in Paris July 14. Sara, too, checked in at Reid Hall from her tour just as the city was celebrating Bastille Day. The Bastille was a hated old fortress in which King Louis XVI jailed citizens who displeased him or his court. When the French Revolution erupted, the first target of the common people was the Bastille. They eventually tore it down.

A sightseeing bus toured the city after dark; Alice and Sara bought tickets and boarded. So much gaiety! Nearly every café boasted a small modern orchestra and people danced on the sidewalks and streets. The fragrance of strong coffee drifted on the air. Celebrators crowded the outdoor tables, drinking and eating rich pastries. Alice's brown eyes must have glinted, watching the "marvelous electric displays...and the gleaming design on the Eiffel Tower."

Always the careful planner, Alice had arranged to visit a cousin, Anna Thomas Welles, and her husband, who lived in Bourre, on the Cher River. Anna had been Alice's classmate at the Towanda school. The Welles were, if not wealthy, well-off. Mr. Welles had come to Europe before Alice was born to build and operate telephone manufacturing factories. He and his wife liked France so much, they stayed in their "typically French" home throughout their retirement.

Alice grinned at the Welles' name for the house where she was a guest. They called it the "new house." This frame structure, painted white, clung to the side of a hill, surrounded by rocks and trees. It was only 100 years old. The huge country house, called a 'chateau' stood close by. The servants lived there, and it had guest rooms, also. Alice regarded the 400-year-old building with apprehension and was glad her luggage had been taken to the new house.

Once settled in, Anna ushered Alice into and around the many caves in the steep hills of this river valley. Long ago, Anna said, sandstone was cut from the cliffs, not from the top, but into the slope of the hill, as in the start of a tunnel. Alice described the caves as "roomy spaces with stone walls, floor, and ceiling. A wall built of stone at the front with a door and one or two small openings for windows plus a chimney were all that were needed for a cozy and durable dwelling!"

Most tourists, her hosts told her, missed seeing these

caves where families had lived for ages. Alice peered at the vine-covered fronts of the dwellings and marveled at how well-concealed they were. The Welles had three caves behind the new house. They used one for a wine cellar, another for a laundry room and another which seemed to be multi-purpose since their children had grown and no longer needed it for a pony stable.

Strolling on the footpaths that led all ways from the house, Alice was enchanted. She inhaled the sweet smell of summer blossoms and saw beauty wherever she looked. Pausing in a mossy glade on the hillside, she could see the glass greenhouses shimmering in the brilliant French sunshine, their interiors a montage of vibrantly - hued flowers.

Places having particularly fine views were graded with decks and comfortable seats. Alice sat and listened to the trickling of narrow little streams that rushed toward several ponds at the base of the hill.

Raising her eyes slightly, she could see the family's vegetable garden across the road and close by the Cher River. There were dwarf apple, peach and nectarine trees, trained to thrive on wooden trellises. All these growing things were surrounded by a high stone wall.

Inside it, strolling one morning, Alice encountered her host. A bit startled, she realized he was picking up snails.

"This is interesting," Alice said, "and a novelty to me." The next thing she knew, she carried two baskets and was picking up snails, too.

The little white ones, Mr. Welles instructed, were to go in one basket, cracked from their shells and fed to the fish in the ponds. The larger, brown snails should be dropped in the other basket, to be starved, and later eaten. Alice said she "...was relieved to learn they would not be ready to cook until after I returned to Paris."

Chapter 17

The Lubeck Affair

"Altogether, it was memorable."
- Alice Evans

Sara Branham and Alice, having unpacked from their respective side trips, probably speculated about Eloise Cram's parallel conference in London as they gaily recounted their own travels and adventures. We can imagine their giggles when Alice told her "snail story".

When the conference opened Alice found her name listed, along with Dr. Robert Buchanan, from Iowa State University, as an official American delegate. And well she should have been. Alice had carried out the president's duties of the American Society of Bacteriologists two years previously, the organization which had appointed her and Dr. Buchanan. She quickly arranged to meet Dr. Buchanan to set their schedules.

Alice looked up another friend, Dr. Rachel Hoffstadt,

also a bacteriologist, from the University of Washington in Seattle. This gave the three women a chance to develop a closer friendship. During the next seven days they enjoyed several social events together.

Only two women graced this First International Congress of Microbiology as officially appointed delegates representing their countries. Alice was one; the other was Dr. Lydia Rabinovich, a Russian, who was held in high esteem for her outstanding research on tuberculosis.

Alice was surprised that Europeans, who were strangers, greeted her affectionately, almost as a relative. Especially those of the Mediterranean countries, she said, "...where brucellosis had caused problems..."

For example, at a crowded reception one night, she met three young Italians, whose English was excellent.

One of them asked, "Will you visit Italy?"

Alice shook her head. "I hope to do that sometime, but not this year."

"You must visit Italy; you have many friends in Italy," he said.

Alice was touched; she had no ties with Italy other than news of her research through the pages of scientific and medical journals. She smiled at the Italian microbiologists and thanked them.

****

Dressed in her best long-waisted dress Alice mingled with the hundreds of guests at a reception in a Parisian palace, recently built in the style of 18th century palaces.

She strolled, drinking in the sight of exquisite furnishings, the great, fragrant bouquets of red roses and gladiolas, and most impressive, the priceless collection of paintings, some of them by Degas. For entertainment, singers from the Opera Comique performed and a famous dance orchestra played popular tunes. The host was one of the organizers of the Congress.

While there, Alice met Professor and Mrs. Olaf Bang. Olaf was the son of the noted Dr. Bernhard Bang, the researcher who discovered brucellosis in cattle. Her spirits soaring, she listened as Professor Bang described his heavy and ongoing research with this disease. Alice's recount of her own thrilling moments of discovery, when she proved that Bernhard's germ and the David Bruce germ were closely related must have been enthralling conversation.

The last big event took place at a theater. Dr. Michel Weinberg, a "native Russian", hosted. He was a member of the Pasteur Institute, and a friend of the President of France. As a gesture of good will, the President offered his opera box to Dr. Weinberg, who invited Alice and four others to join him. They saw Tannhauser on the vast stage. Alice could not contain her amazement when six gigantic draft horses pulled wagons across the stage as the first act ended.

In her Memoirs Alice straightforwardly wrote about the rest of the evening. Afterwards, on this balmy July night, she related that Dr. Weinberg first walked her and Mme. Lydia Rabinovich, to Lydia's hostel, near the Louvre.

From there, the doctor and Alice strolled across the Place de la Concorde and its design of lights. They boarded the subway; got off at Montparnasse Station and walked toward the glowing lights and music of the cafés on the boulevard. From there they sauntered to Reid Hall, talking about the controversy being argued in the Congress, no doubt. Perhaps they spoke of Alice's impressions of France, or their mutual microbe-hunting friends. It must have been an enchanted night, in spite of Alice's matter-of-fact description.

There are no records to show if Alice and Michel ever met again but this strong, quiet man remained in her memory for the rest of her life.

As for what transpired in the Congress, the most important subject appeared to be the controversy about the anti-tuberculosis vaccine, called B.C.G. The "B" for bacillus, "C" and "G" for the names of the researchers, Calmette and Guerin, of the Pasteur Institute.

Their flammable topic of debate dealt with the tubercular deaths of 68 German babies in the early summer of 1930. The vaccine used for the infants' inoculations came from the Pasteur Institute, which was being pressed to accept the blame for somehow having sent bad vaccine to the town of Lubeck. Calmette defended the vaccine in his scheduled address at the Congress. He explained his theory of causing immunity with live bacilli. There was no danger, he said, of non-virulent (laboratory treated) bacilli becoming poisonous after being administered to humans. The tragedy happened, he said, because someone at the Institute made a mistake and sent virulent vaccines to Lubeck. He pointed out the thousands of "good" shots given European babies with not a single case of tuberculosis reported.

A contrary opinion came from an American medical doctor, S.A. Petroff, who contended that the bacillus may turn poisonous under certain conditions in the human body, possibly producing tuberculosis. Many Americans there agreed with him. Alice, while remaining impartial, felt the bitterness permeate the air as men's voices grew loud and angry. Many other subjects had to be addressed during the session, and the issue was not resolved.

Investigation unraveled a tale of disaster. Calmette's belief in his vaccine proved correct, for the blame did lie with the hospital laboratory which produced the vaccines. Tubercle bacilli and Calmette's vaccine were made "side by side", and due to human error, the virulent human cultures were switched with the attenuated. Two men in charge of the laboratory went to jail, and the laboratory was declared by the court to be unfit for such work.

Later that week Alice sat at a lunch table in Versailles, France, smiling and trying hard to converse with a charming Italian man at her right. Alice spoke no Italian; the gentleman, Dr. Azzi, a member of the congress, spoke halting English. With considerable charm he made an effort to become acquainted.

"Is your man a bacteriologist?" he said.

"I have no husband," Alice said. "I am a bacteriologist myself."

Dr. Azzi gazed at a far wall while he put together his next English words.

"If you would give me your name, I might know who you are," he said.

Alice dug in her purse and gave him her card.

A huge smile broke over his face. "Ah! I did not imaginate that it was you!" Dr. Azzi said.

They became friends and remained so for many years through correspondence. Dr. Azzi was the editor of an Italian journal, a review magazine of microbiological subjects. The luncheon ended the First International Congress of Microbiology, and what a week it had been!

Chapter 18

Going Abroad

*"Give her the fruit of her hands,
and let her own works praise her
in the gates."*
- Proverbs 31:31

Two years passed. Undulant fever lay dormant and Alice felt well. She made lists and bought new clothes and planned a precise schedule, this spring of 1932, that would start with another trip across the Atlantic. Due her were four weeks of vacation time which she would use to tour Great Britain.

The remaining six weeks of work-study she was to spend in a laboratory of the National Institute for Medical Research in Hempstead, on the outskirts of London. Dr. McCoy, ever watchful for opportunities to enrich the lives of his medical family, arranged for Alice to carry on her streptococci studies in this institute. She had worked more or less continually on streptococci since the early 1920's. What a career enhancement! Such a vacation opportunity!

Ida Bengtson again accompanied Alice on the outbound journey. The two women toured southern England, including Stonehenge. Then Ida, who was along strictly for a holiday, waved good-by and took off for the continent.

Alice checked in at the Institute. She quickly met investigators who were part of a team intent on streptococcal problems. Alice said she was "stimulated" when she met Mrs. Ethel Christie, and others, who came to the laboratory more than a few times to bring freshly isolated strains of streptococci.

Alice put together a collection of strains for herself. Unable to do more than a cursory examination, she sorted them out. They provided the base for a future study of streptococci.

A highlight of her summer in Hempstead was meeting Welsh-born Ben Davies. Ben was an executive director in charge of education about dairy products. During the past two years Ben found that English dairymen opposed pasteurization as firmly as did their American counterparts. He was making slow progress trying to convince the industry that raw milk could be dangerous. One day, newspapers published a story about the child of a "distinguished" English family who had come down with brucellosis. Tragically, a severe bone infection followed. Ben went on to relate that this child had drunk nothing but certified milk. Worse yet, this milk came from a herd owned by a rich, well-known person. Newspapers made much of the incident, and Ben said, wryly, that the demand quickly increased for pasteurized milk.

Alice charmed Mr. and Mrs. Davies. Their "common

interest in dairy problems" started a long-lasting friendship and the Davies entertained Alice often while she was in England that summer of 1932. Being fussed over made the six weeks of study fly by for her.

Almost magically, Alice found herself on the train to Glenmorganshire, Wales, to visit relatives. Life could not have been sweeter for this country-born traveler. Certainly she deserved the reward of special training and a vacation.

In contrast, there were others, veterans of World War I, who suffered horribly this worst year of our country's Great Depression. In June these United States veterans with their wives and children marched on Washington, D.C. They moved into vacant shanties below the capitol building, and along the Anacostia River. They were destitute, ill-clothed, hungry. They needed the bonus money promised them by the federal government to be paid this year, immediately.

State troupers and soldiers met the protesters, burned the shacks and threw tear gas bombs at the 15,000 veterans and their families. President Hoover said they were overtly lawless. The war heroes were now the object of contempt; some government officials began rumors saying that they were "thieves, plug-uglies, degenerates", not really veterans at all. Many citizens of Virginia, when the little ragged army passed through, refused them food and even water. "You're rebels," they cried. "The president said so."

The Bonus Army dispersed, worse off than before they came.

In July, President Hoover approved the pitifully inadequate Emergency Relief and Construction Act. When Franklin Roosevelt became President the next year, he began a "reform program," which he described as

160

"...organized for self-help...". Two of these programs were the Civilian Conservation Corps and the Works Progress Administration. They gave jobs to about two and a half million grateful men, until World War II.

The Great Depression dragged on. Poverty thrived, weakening its victims, making them vulnerable to disease. Streptococci grew to be a deadly reality as Alice continued her study of the organism in England in 1936. Dr. McCoy arranged for Alice to work that summer with two London bacteriologists, Griffith and Chapneys, who were researching streptococci subjects "closely related" to hers.

Alice and Sara Branham boarded a slow freight ship to England. It had passenger cabins and was cheaper than the luxury liners plying the Atlantic. Since the Institute did not pay transportation for its employees, Alice and Sara decided to leave early and spend the money they saved on ship passage for a room in a small hotel. It was near the University College, where the Second International Congress of Microbiology was to be held.

Again, this was a combination of work and play. Alice met Sir Weldon Dalrymple-Champneys whose reports on Brucella abortus she had read and studied. He treated her to lunch at the Guard's Club. (Champneys was an officer in the English Grenadiers.) During their conversation, Alice queried him on what was happening in the Italian-Ethiopian War. A prelude to World War II it had broken out while Alice was steaming along to England on the mail boat which had no communication system.

Much of the pre-conference time Alice spent exchanging information with Drs. Griffith and Dalrymple-Champneys. In years to come, both in war and peacetime, the two microbiologists would correspond with each other about

161

brucellosis.

Because Sara and Alice had worked together on meningococci for many years at the National Institute of Health they were both intrigued to meet Dr. W.M. Scott, who was "an authority on meningococci." The two women went to dinner at the Scotts' home. Five years later, during the Second World War, Alice was shocked and grieved to learn that both Dr. Griffith and Dr. Scott had been killed during a bombing raid in London.

Alice wrote several paragraphs in her Memoirs, describing her contact with the then elderly Dr. John Eyre. It is apparent Alice held Dr. Eyre in high regard, not so much for his impressive home, but for his character. (True, the mansion was situated on a richly historic street in London, where the statue of Joseph Lister stands to remind bacteriologists of their heritage). Eyre, more than thirty years before, in medical journals, had credited Mary Bruce's heroic work as a pioneer microbiologist. Alice stressed in her Memoirs that it was mainly due to Mary Bruce's persistence that the subject of Malta fever ever became an issue. The resulting causal organism, named the Bruce bacillus, Alice said, ... "was a brilliant chapter in the history of infectious diseases." If Alice basked in the glow of Mary Bruce's late-given glory, it is understandable. In 1936, Alice was receiving recognition for her discovery of the relationship of the two microbes, and their impact on human suffering. Women's Medical College had bestowed an honorary medical degree upon her, a fact that went unnoticed by many medical males. She had been given well – placed and favorable publicity as her discovery was confirmed all over the world. Alice had brought fame to the National Institute of Health!

A guest for tea at the Eyre mansion on Portland Place one afternoon, Alice found that Dr. Eyre was "intensely interested" in the contribution the United States was making to the study of brucellosis, no matter which animal it affected - cattle, hogs, goats or any other animal, including humans. Alice relaxed, fascinated, viewing a beautiful collection of old china, while John Eyre spun stories of his life as a young physician being sent to Malta in the Mediterranean to investigate the deathly fevers English army and navy men were contracting.

He told of working with David Bruce on the Malta Fever Commission. A group photograph taken in 1904 of British Malta Fever Commissioners shows Dr. Eyre seated to the right of Dr. David Bruce. Eyre, whose dark hair is receding, wears a light-colored three-piece-suit and appears to be a very small man. We study the other men in the picture, who also seem undersized. Center front, looms David Bruce, his heavy hair combed flat and his big, waxed mustache curling up on the ends. At 49 he's a bit jowly. A watch chain hangs across his wide, vested middle. Understanding dawns. The commission is staffed by average-sized men. Bruce is a giant of a man.

Continuing his story Dr. Eyre said that the biggest news of the Commission was that infected goats caused human bacterial infections and that it was transmitted through the goat's milk. Alice, of course, was familiar with the story and delighted in hearing it told by a participant.

A few days later, Mrs. Eyre, with chauffeur, drove to the women's modest hotel and picked up Alice and Sara. They motored to Oxford, had lunch and a fine day sightseeing. No taking the bus or walking London's shopping district! Not only were the bacteriologists being

163

wined and dined, they were being tea-ed and lunched!

Alice wrote, "It seemed as if Dr. And Mrs. Eyre had appointed themselves a committee of two to make the visit a memorable one for me."

The middle-aged little woman from the wandering Pennsylvania hills must have been slightly a-tremble. Did her feelings belie the sensible words of her recollections later? Here she was, on her third trip abroad, being courted by aristocracy. The Eyres gave a dinner in Alice's honor at the splendid Royal Societies Club, where Alice was seated next to medical men active in brucellosis work.

Prominent among them was Dr. I. Forest Huddleson. Alice saw him as a man of medium stature, with sparse brown hair, lively gray eyes and a pipe clamped in the corner of his mouth. He seemed reserved unless he was discussing bacteriology. Then with a sudden smile and quick gestures Dr. Huddleson described his fatigue, frustration and final victory in producing an "instant" test for detecting brucellosis. Dr. Huddleson worked at a "cow college", Michigan Agricultural College in East Lansing, Michigan. Years later, John Hannah, president of this college, which was to become Michigan State University, stated that Dr. Huddleson and his research gave "more value to humanity than a football team."

Alice wrote of Dr. Huddleson, that he "…had made and continued to make a great contribution to the knowledge of brucellosis…"

Dr. and Mrs. Scott and, of course, Sara and other scientists made for stimulating dinner talk.

The icing on the entertainment cake came after the fancy meal. The International Congress hosted a reception at the London Museum, which once had been a private estate. There, Alice delighted in seeing "friends and acquaintances" whom she had met at the first Congress in Paris. We wonder if the trio of warm-hearted Italians were there to remind her that she would "always have friends in Italy."

Perhaps because of their mutual and humble Welsh beginnings, her new friends, the Davies, had a special place in Alice's heart. Ben Davies was still a director in the United Dairies Company. He began his career as a truck driver, a lad fresh from Wales, and worked up the administrative ladder. Alice had a comfortable, happy time with Mr. and Mrs. Davies at dinner in their home, then as if to outdo themselves, they gave a dinner party for 28 at the Savoy Hotel honoring Alice. Sara was invited, along with other Americans, dairy company people and Dr. and Mrs. G.H. Wilson. Alice pointedly mentioned being impressed with meeting Doctors Orla-Jenson, Hansen and Olaf Bang. Dancing and an illusion entertainer followed.

The extracurricular activities ended with Alice being taken on a tour of the United Dairies main laboratories. She found herself being handed out of a gorgeous new, blue car and ushered into the building. She looked about, as spellbound as Alice in Wonderland. These laboratories, in contrast to her own simple workspace, shouted luxury, with expensive pieces of equipment and parqueted wood floors. The offices and library glowed in shades of blue with soft blue wool rugs, and furniture and books upholstered in fine leather, also blue.

Upon leaving, dazzled by the opulence, Alice signed a special page in the front of the guest book. On the line just above her name, Alice saw with a thrill of surprise the signature of her old teacher and friend from Wisconsin, Dr.

Elmer McCollum. She noted from the date that he had been there several weeks earlier.

Alice had two vivid memories of this Second International Congress for scientists. One was that she gave two informal talks on infectious diseases, which were unscheduled. Alice had scant minutes to think what she would say, but the members enthusiastically accepted her impromptu speech about the high incidence of unrecognized chronic brucella infection "in areas where the disease is prevalent."

Her second recollection was one of pride in Hans Zinsser as he presided over the section covering brucellae. He did it, Alice said, "with such distinction in knowledge, skill, and grace." She was not one to let the disagreement she had with Zinsser, years before, color her admiration for him now.

Star-crossed Dr. W.N. Scott presided over the streptococci session. Alice found it "stimulating", especially when Dr. Scott asked her to enter his discussion.

The Congress ended with a banquet on Friday evening. At the dinner hall door, Alice received a numbered card, indicating her place at one of the tables. She found her spot and discovered it was beside Dr. Alexander Fleming, who discovered a forerunner of antibiotic medicine, penicillin, in 1928! Dr. Fleming graciously kept up a running commentary on the strictly formal (and to Alice, oddly funny) British tradition of professional toastmaster. Alice left the conference with "Hear Ye! Hear Ye!" ringing in her head. Maybe as she rode to the airport she worried about her first airplane trip, ever.

Chapter 19

Holland, Famous Persons and Retirement

"Dr. Evans, ...you are one of the most wonderful women of our age..."
- Carrie Chapman Catt

"As we approached the Netherlands, we were flying at an altitude of 1600 feet, I was entranced on discovering that I could see at a glance enough of the coastline to identify its features with those on a map I was holding."

How she must have tingled on her first airplane ride! Few travelers used airlines in those early aviation years. Yet, there she flew, at a breathtaking 350 feet over the lowlands, toward Amsterdam. She looked down as a bird might have done that clear day. She saw well-squared fields bounded by ditches dug to connect with larger canals, and bridges everywhere. Cattle ranged, and as the engine propellers roared toward the town of Gouda, she spied what she guessed were plots of gladiolas, splendid in their shades of red and yellow.

An unexpected bonanza came to Alice because of her attendance at the International Congress. Many professional and social contacts Alice made during these days were with scientists from the Netherlands and Belgium. When she mentioned her plans to visit as a tourist, her new acquaintances had gotten busy. A stranger, Alice found herself welcomed everywhere, thanks to the bacteriologists' "grapevine." She enjoyed tours guided by scientists she never would have known about otherwise.

Delft, an old western town in Netherlands, Alice said, "...was a high point of interest." She arrived, and upon verifying that an interesting-looking building was indeed the home of Dr. Albert Jan Kluyver, she tucked her address book back into her purse. After knocking at the door of the residence, Alice was ushered into the dining room of the Kluyvers. They had a guest that early afternoon, and Alice soon became acquainted with him. He was Dutch, presently teaching at Stanford University, and had taken an advanced degree, studying under Dr. Kluyver.

She met the handsome Kluyver children and their gracious mother.

The two men then took Alice on a three-hour walk through the ancient city. They strolled on sidewalks bordered by trees and canals and very old brick houses, stopping, she said, "...wherever there was a memento of the great naturalist, Leeuwenhoek, who initiated the science of microbiology when, using one of his microscopes, he discovered yeast cells." Leeuwenhoek had lived out his life in Delft, manufacturing microscopes and using them to search for origins of just about every substance he could lay his hands on.

When the little group ended their tour at the tomb of Leeuwenhoek, in the 15th century Old Church, they went back for tea, which Mrs. Kluyver had waiting for them in the living room.

Afterwards, the doctor showed her his upstairs offices and laboratory.

Alice crawled into her bed that night in her hotel room, bone-tired.

On to Ghent, Belgium. Alice said "...I knew no one in the city..." Yet, when she checked in at her hotel, the clerk handed her a note, signed Prof. Van de Velde. The professor was head of biochemistry and bacteriology at the University of Ghent, and he would call for her the following morning.

Alice freshened and reveled in the wonderful sense of fellowship she was experiencing on these trips to Europe. Downstairs in the hotel's dining room she was hardly more than seated when a waiter presented her with a magnificent bouquet of "...dahlias and gladiolas, both of a rich, red shade, pink roses and maidenhair fern. They were from Prof. Van de Velde's garden."

The next day was Saturday. Alice was more than ready when the professor arrived mid-morning with his assistant, Dr. Margaret Hauwaerte. Alice deemed this most thoughtful, for the professor's English was limited. The lady doctor did speak good English; she had studied at Columbia University for three years.

The two scientists took Alice on a walking tour. They visited the University of Ghent, considered to be modern since it had been founded in 1816. In a new science building, Alice looked about, impressed at the beautifully equipped laboratories where routine and investigative work was pursued. Reverently she touched the original leather upholstered chair of the famous organic chemist, Kekule, remembering her sometimes dry college chemistry courses, and marveling that history was coming alive for her. Perhaps Kekule had worked from this very chair after he awoke from his world-renowned dream in which he saw a string of atoms put together like a snake swallowing its own tail. From this vision he went on to formulate the principle of the benzene ring.

On the way out, Alice was asked to sign an honored guest book. Curious, she glanced at the last name on the register. It was the signature of her fighting brucellosis friend from Dayton, Ohio, Dr. Walter Simpson!

Alice met interesting persons at home, too. A letter she kept for sentimental reasons came from a reigning movie star, Marie Dressler. It was dated January 23, 1934.

My dear Dr. Evans:

I cannot tell you the great esteem I have for you and for your wonderful work. Thank you so very much for your lovely wishes inscribed in Paul de Kruif's book, "Men Against Death."

I shall look forward to meeting you so that I can thank you personally.

Sincerely and gratefully,

Marie Dressler

In an explanatory note written later, Alice said: "Marie Dressler visited National Institutes of Health sometime around 1933. It was after she had learned that she had a fatal disease, I believe. She greatly admired the work N.I.H. was doing. Some of us met her.

"Later, after she had become an invalid, Paul de Kruif conceived the idea of sending her a copy of his recently published <u>Men Against Death</u>. He asked those of us whose work he had discussed in the book to inscribe it and include a brief message to Miss Dressler."

Cancer, the "fatal disease", claimed Miss Dressler. She had won the Oscar Award for the 1930 movie, <u>Min and Bill</u>, and only a year earlier, had starred in two movies, <u>Tugboat Annie</u> and <u>Dinner at Eight</u>; both were outstandingly successful.

Another letter which Alice saved, came just before the Christmas holiday in 1935. Alice opened her laboratory mail and pulled out letterhead stationery from Mount Sinai Hospital in New York. Scanning to the signature, she saw with surprise and pleasure it was from the noted researcher, Bela Schick. She had met him and his wife at the First International Congress in Paris.

For decades, Dr. Schick had been probing diseases of children. He delved so deeply into investigations of scarlet fever, that the world knew him as an authority for that disease. When he had left his Hungarian birthplace to work with Dr. Von Pirquet in Vienna, he became the father of medicine's knowledge of allergy and serum sickness. He struggled with researching the elusive infantile diarrhea disease, and tuberculosis. Mostly, he was famous for the skin test he developed to determine if a person were likely to catch diphtheria.

Starting in 1914, public health nurses and doctors set up camp in schools and administered the Schick test during epidemics of diphtheria. Children, grimacing and groaning, felt a needle slide under the skin of their arm, and a tiny amount of toxin released. After a few days, the medical team inspected. A red, inflamed-looking reaction meant that this little body had been exposed to diphtheria. There followed, then, three more injections of an antitoxin, a week apart.

The good Dr. Schick, now a pediatrician at Mount Sinai Hospital, needed a different kind of serum. He asked Alice for "a small quantity of convalescent goat serum for a child ill with undulant fever."

Alice was honored by his request. We can see her dropping everything to package the miracle medicine and post it in the return mail.

****

Streptococcus was the scarlet fever germ that had nearly caused Alice's death as a child. She came in job contact with one of the many types of streptococci as early as 1918, when the Department of Agriculture ran a study of "good" streptococci that were used in cheese ripening. She would leave this streptococcus for a time, then return to study the "bad" disease-causing strains. Alice wrote two chapters in Memoirs about her streptococci research. She seemed to regard this work as fascinating as the brucellosis puzzle. The results were not as far-reaching, but Alice's method of serological typing in the classification of streptococci was an important contribution to bacteriology.

In 1936 the United States began to pull itself up from the crushing poverty of the Great Depression. The federal government had passed the Social Security Act a few months before and, in an unusual but brilliant act of farsightedness, allocated a portion of these funds to the National Institute of Health for medical research. With the new monies, more microbiologists hired in at N.I.H. and Margaret Pittman was one of them.

She was born in Arkansas in 1901 to a "...horse and buggy doctor who passionately served all people," Margaret described her father. Her mother, a cousin of inventor Cyrus McCormick, could repair things mechanical, sewed expertly, painted with oils, kept a lending library, promoted education and taught piano playing.

Margaret leaned toward a career in medicine after her first experience of administering ether. While her father prepared to set a bone fracture on a patient, Margaret poured ether over cotton cloth, draped it across an egg beater and held the contraption over the patient's nose.

At Arkansas' Hendrix College she majored in mathematics and biology, graduated magna cum laud and worked for two years as principal and teacher at the Academy of Galloway Female College, also in her home state. She saved as much money as possible for Margaret's goal was to prepare for, she said, "some form of medical work." She was quickly accepted at the University of Chicago graduate school in 1925. There she studied bacteriology and hygiene, working part-time to add to her savings. Miraculously, she said, "A few months before I was to receive the M.S. degree, the department offered me a fellowship to continue my studies for a Ph.D., an opportunity undreamed of."

Elated, she took medical school courses and in 1928 left the University of Chicago for the Rockefeller Institute for Medical Research in New York. Her project there was to "determine if <u>Haemophilis influenzae</u> is the cause of influenza." This germ was a bacterium and caused an infection, both of which Margaret Pittman investigated. (Research then had not uncovered the fact that influenza is caused by a virus.)

She joined N.I.H. in 1936 where she was warmly greeted by Sara Branham. Dr. Branham had been one of her instructors at the University of Chicago. Margaret met Alice, who had researched meningococci in 1918-19 and the 20's and was presently immersed in streptococci experiments.

Margaret's orders were to develop a potency test for the meningococcus antiserum that would be more dependable than the injections which had been used in previous meningitis epidemics. She worked on this project briefly, for Sara Branham, we remember, discovered the combination cure of sulfanilomides and the horse antiserum in treating meningitis.

Margaret turned to new research - particularly the <u>Bordetella pertussis</u> (whooping cough) vaccine and rose steadily up the ranks of N.I.H., excelling at everything she focused upon.

Seventeen years later she became one of the first women with the title, "Chief" of a laboratory at N.I.H. In the words of Dr. Victoria Harden, Director of the N.I.H. Historical Office and DeWitt Stetten, Jr. Museum of Medical Research, who became Margaret's friend later, "...She [Pittman] had an international scientific reputation. I had asked her once whether a male with such a reputation would have had to wait twenty years to be named lab chief. She replied, 'Well, I never let it bother me.'"

Through the years Margaret Pittman was given

174

recognition and honored for her contributions to research in respiratory infections, conjunctivitis and meningitis, and the regulation and standardization of bacterial vaccines and toxins, particularly stressing pertussis as a toxin-mediated disease. The Committee on the Status of Women in Microbiology awarded Miss Pittman the Alice Evans Award in 1990. This award had been established to honor Alice as first lady of microbiology.

Today, Margaret Pittman, at 92 years of age, continues her career as a Guest Worker after having "retired" from Federal Service at age 70. She maintains her office in the Division of Biologic Standards and the FDA Center for Drugs and Biologics...."And I still have my own parking space," she said.

Chapter 20

Leaving the Laboratory

*"...If your mind is lively you will
soon find other interests..."*
– Cardine Lejeune

We remember that after Alice fell victim to chronic undulant fever, Dr. McCoy steered her toward other inquiries.

During this time, the National Health Service separated from the Treasury Department. The previous year, the National Institute of Health had moved to nearby suburban Bethesda, Maryland. In the summer of 1939, Alice received a letter from the Secretary of Treasury, Henry Morgenthau, Jr. He expressed appreciation for her work as "Senior Bacteriologist". Alice, in precise handwriting, made a notation at the bottom of Morgenthau's letter, indicating that the cabinet member "owned a dairy farm in New York state."

One January day in 1939, Alice picked up a copy of the Washington Evening Star. A reproduced photograph, captioned, "This is believed to be the first girls' basketball team, the 1903 squad at Kansas University," drew her attention.

Alice, of course, knew better, and so did all her former teammates and their competitors, Elmira College in New York and Mansfield Normal School in Pennsylvania. (Continuing the search for several years, she found a statement made by the Cleveland Plain Dealer offering that girls started throwing baskets in earnest in 1912).

Going even further, Alice cites two references in her Memoirs. In the first, Curti and Carstensen's The University of Wisconsin: A History, 1848-1925, she discovered a photographic plate depicting the 1897 Women's Basketball Team. Later, she said she "ran across" something that predates this by about two years.

"In a Memorial Service, honoring Dr. Martha Tracy, Dean of the Women's Medical College of Pennsylvania, from 1918 to 1940, Dr. Marian Edwards Park gave tribute. She was president of Byrn Mawr College at the time of the ceremony (1942). Dr. Tracy and Dr. Park had been classmates at Byrn Mawr, where they graduated in 1898. In her memorial comments Dr. Park mentioned that Martha Tracy was captain of the class basketball team for three years."

Then in characteristic Alice Evans non-judgmental style, she ends the discussion, writing," This may not be the earliest date of women's basketball."

Alice had to leave off her research of live brucellosis cases around 1939, and returned to work only with the killed microbe. Then she started a new chapter in her career with the study of beta-hemolytic streptococci, group A. Her directive: to develop a therapeutic antiserum. The miraculous age of antibiotics was beginning. By 1940 penicillin and sulfa compounds were in general use. Alice said, ..."when the cures were found (the antibiotics), it seemed like a dream had come true... but there were other problems of streptococcal diseases besides those of therapy, so I continued my studies."

Alice spent a large part of her laboratory days handling hazardous bacteria. It gave her more than a "sobering sense of responsibility", especially after her last violent attack of undulant fever in 1943. With orders to begin work on a serum against streptococci, came a "buoyant" feeling, she said.

This bacterium, although dangerous as a human disease, posed no threat in the laboratory. One just took the usual precautions. It was with a lighter heart, then, that Alice tackled what she called bacteriophage. The term means, in this study, that there are streptococci susceptible to destruction by other bacteria.

Alice said she would set up an experiment with these bacteriophages in the afternoon, and see results as soon as she examined the experiment the next morning. She had fun one day when she tired of a tedious routine and lumped all the strains together. In the morning, she gleefully discovered that it had worked better than the original process.

She compared this research, in some ways, with that of Alexander Fleming. When someone questioned him about how he had discovered penicillin, he explained that he had been "just playing."

Scientists discovered and named some thirty types of

streptococci during this time in her career. By the end of another six years, researchers had discovered sixteen more types. These, plus the drugs sulfa and penicillin, provided an exciting addition to the fight against disease.

Adding to her adventures of the 1940's, Alice recounted in her memoirs the honor of being named an "outstanding woman" by the Woman's Centennial Congress. Carrie Chapman Catt, Chairwoman of this Congress, informed her that Cornell University made the recommendation. By "outstanding woman," the organization meant a woman who was working in an area impossible to enter in the 1890's. Mrs. Catt asked Alice to attend the celebration in New York City as a special guest. Each chosen visitor received a "commemorative gift" of a book entitled, Victory - How Women Won It, published by the National Women's Suffrage Association.

About the occasion, Alice said, "I was unable to attend the New York celebration. The book was received and it is a cherished treasure."

"In May, 1941, the General Federation of Women's Clubs celebrated their 50th Anniversary in Atlantic City, and they carried the theme of the Woman's Centennial Congress. I attended the meeting..."

Alice felt singularly honored when the Status of Women in Microbiology Committee set up the Alice Evans award. Recognition was coming her way.

BETHESDA, MARYLAND
1945-1975

Nineteen forty-five arrived and on September 2, World War II, history's costliest war in both human lives and property, ended with Japan's surrender. Alice rejoiced with friends and co-workers. She had another reason to celebrate. In just 26 days she would retire from her career as a senior bacteriologist.

Good-looking, ruddy-faced Dr. Parran, Surgeon General of National Health Service and hero of the new aggressive public health movement, was host for the recognition dinner. More that 100 invitations were mailed to honorees. Alice, now 64 years old, shared the honors with her dear friend, Ida Bengtson.

At the head table Alice was seated to the left of Dr. Parran, Ida to his right. James Leake, about whom Alice wrote so fondly in Memoirs, and Sara Branham were also at his table along with Mrs. Luke Wilson, who had deeded valuable property to N.I.H.

What went on inside Alice's heart as she heard the smiling praise of her colleagues? Did her steady scientist's hand quiver when she accepted the lovingly given gifts? When she exchanged glances with Ida, did she see through unshed tears? Both women, never married, had made science the center of their lives. Were they already feeling left out?

Those last days before leaving her laboratory and office were bittersweet. Gone would be the hiss of Bunson burners. No more juggling sterile cotton in one hand while heating a needle red-hot with the other. Missing, too, the sweet odor of the acid, phenol, used to sterilize worktables. She would even miss the clink of Petrie dish lids.

This same year, at age 57, Sara Branham married Philip Matthews who lived across the road from a house Sara had had built in 1941 or '42 in Bethesda. There had been an orchard on the lot and Margaret Pittman remembers tying on an apron and helping Sara can apples. Philip died, Margaret said, "when he and Sara had been married only four years."

Sara continued to work using her maiden name. Records show she researched and reported on studies with Sadie A. Carlin and Karl Habel, and among other scientific papers, wrote a section on meningitis for the Encyclopedia Britannica. The Schlesinger Library notes that the titles of her many published papers and books were received in 1956.

Yes, Alice's friend, "Sally" was a unique person. She managed to instill a late, if brief, romance into her life. She was happy to be part of N.I.H., as were Alice, Ida Bengtson, Eloise Cram, Sadie Carlin, Margaret Pittman and other notable female bacteriologists. They received encouragement from their chiefs and though their pay was not equal to male workers doing the same job, at least these women had careers. Businesses and universities usually did not hire women scientists. That left the Public Health Service open to receive the new "career women". ..."In that sense," Dr. Harden said, "the federal government was far ahead of academia (as it was with racial, ethnic and religious minorities, somewhat later.)"

For Alice, retirement meant a decent pension and a well deserved rest from the alarm clock. Thankfully, she had not had a disabling attack of brucellosis in the last two years and in time, she left chronic symptoms behind.

Reflecting on other past honors given her, Alice was pleased with the honorary Medical Degree she received from what is now Medical College of Pennsylvania. Wilson College had awarded her a Doctor of Science Degree as did the University of Wisconsin.

Retirement gave Alice time to indulge in her favorite hobby, reading. She continued to roam about searching for lithographs. She got the opportunity to travel, this time south of the United States border as a delegate for the Inter-American Committee on Brucellosis.

Alice served this group for several years as president. When members first told her she had been appointed, Alice told friends she was stunned. She flew to Mexico City for the Fifth Congress of this Committee the year after her retirement. There she found she had been elected president of the committee on brucellosis! Within three days, the committee had drawn up their goals. One was "to interest the emerging world health organizations to establish an international committee on brucellosis, and among other things, to start a bulletin on brucellosis which could be quickly transmitted between countries."

Indulging herself, Alice arranged to spend six weeks in Mexico. The Congress came first, of course, and Alice read her paper, <u>Brucellosis in the United States, Past, Present and Future</u>. She did not expect the lively and controversial discussion which followed her talk. She had quoted the famous French scientist, Nicolle, as saying brucellosis was "a disease of the future." This meant to him that the disease brought out delayed and/or hidden symptoms and chronic manifestations. Alice, and many others, translating his remark, believed he meant that there would be..." an

world, especially as they pertained to public health. Sometimes she picked up her pen and protested or suggested. Usually, because of her stature in the scientific community, she got a speedy reply.

Alice lived independently, on her own financial resources, until she was 85. At this time, she applied for Medicare. The year was 1966, and Medicare forms required that she swear she had no affiliation to the Communist Party. With quiet emphasis, Alice refused, declaring it denied her a constitutional right. So workers pushed through the application anyway, without her signature. Certainly, if anyone in the nation was entitled to benefits, it was this laboratory researcher who had suffered so much at the whims of job-related chronic disease.

One early spring day Alice sorted her mail and found a letter from her former teacher and friend, Elmer McCollum. Typically, he addressed her as "Miss Evans," writing:

"It seems a long time since I heard from you. I have often thought of you through the years and have held you in great esteem, first, because of your friendliness and engaging smile, which still lives in memory...

...I retired from my professorship in the school of Hygiene and Public Health in 1946...In April of 1945...I was opened for surgery on my large intestine...and I did not expect to survive. But after a year, I was of the opinion that I should be around for some time, so set up a laboratory in the greenhouse on the main campus (Johns Hopkins University) and began to read old books and journals to take notes of the writing of a History of Nutrition. This occupied me for ten years. The book was published in November 1957, by

Houghton Mifflin Co. It has not sold very well, but the 16 reviews which I have seen were so good that I am glad I wrote it.

...With but one-sixth vision I am somewhat handicapped, but I still do an immense amount of reading in the progress of organic and biochemistry and microbiology. I read only with a magnifying glass and perfect illumination. But being now in my 83rd year, it is likely I shall be blind within a few years.

...I have had a wonderful life. Both the University of Wisconsin and Johns Hopkins afforded me the opportunity to do whatever I wanted to do, including resources for as much experimental work as time would permit. I look back with much pleasure to my associations with enthusiastic young people...my days are still eventful and my skies bright.

...I wish you the best of everything. With warm personal regards,

Sincerely,

Elmer V. McCollum
Professor Emeritus of Biochemistry"

Alice replied with fellow-feeling.

"I was very pleased to receive your letter. It is a long time since we have chanced to meet at a scientific meeting, and I knew nothing about your serious illness and other news about yourself. You are rising nobly above your handicaps. There would be no 'problem of the aged' if all were like you.

I, too, am an octogenarian who can look back on an interesting life. Like you, I was fortunate to work under chiefs who gave their own inclinations. And they supported me when the going got rough, as it sometimes did.

It seems that my role as a scientist was not to chart new paths into the unknown, as you did with the vitamins, but to sense discrepancies, call attention to them and do what I could to make corrections.

I am fairly spry for my age, though I have to rest two or three times a day if I do anything energetic. I am fortunate enough to have practically normal sight and hearing, I read a good deal and attend occasional lectures, theater, opera, etc. I try to follow new developments in the field in which I was active. Also, in recent years, my interest in international affairs had occupied considerable time.

That I would become aroused again to take part in another brucellosis controversy did not enter my mind until an incident occurred which I could not allow to pass without a protest. I have long been interested in the plight of chronic brucellosis patients. Because objective signs of disease are vague and diagnostic tests are unreliable, the diagnosis used to be 'neurasthenia' almost invariably. But now, since disability compensation has become available to many sufferers from this largely occupational disease, the chronic patients are commonly accused of malingering.

Perhaps, at my age, with no official backing, my protests may seem futile, but sometime the truth will be recognized, and I am hoping that my efforts will help to bring about that recognition.

The problem is old, but the unreasonableness of the doctors' attitude was magnified when all sixteen of the brucellosis patients at Fort Detrick, who failed to recover fully from their brucella infections contracted in the line of duty, had their reputations impaired by a blanket indictment of the group as malingerers or psychoneurotics prior to infection.

How ironical to blame the patients for prolonged illness! The tendency of brucellosis to incapacitate men and animals for long periods must have been the feature of this disease which led to its inclusion among those studied for possible use in germ warfare.

After seeing the announcement of your <u>History of Nutrition</u>, I obtained a copy at the National Medical Library where I do my professional reading. I was particularly interested in refreshing my mind on your contributions to the discovery of vitamins, because you were deep in those studies the year I was a member of your class of graduate students. I have often thought about your generosity of time given to the class when your research work must have been exciting and demanding. The class could not have been inspiring, for as I remember, not one of the four members showed indication of becoming a research biochemist.

With kindest regards and best wishes."

She enclosed a copy of her 1948 publication, <u>Brucellosis and Its Implications</u>. In 1967, Alice learned of McCollum's death.

Alice had fallen to the last disabling attack of undulant fever in 1943. Twenty-one years of battling with an unseen enemy; an enemy who chose its own times and weapons. Each time, from 1922 onward, (she suffered five serious and extended bouts of the fever in as many hospitals) she returned to her beloved laboratory, buttoned her lab coat,

190

and although weakened, was determined to learn as much about this chronic disease as she could. Once, she had been bedridden for 14 months.

She had studied in her hospital room, angry that those reporting on brucellosis seemed to be eager to accuse chronic sufferers of pretending to be sick in order to claim disability benefits.

Dr. M.L. Hughes, back in 1897, defended the Malta soldiers, saying that the "neurotic" symptoms which often follow a brucellosis attack, are indeed, caused by the disease. Yet, 74 years later, the same accusations of malingering were being cast at laboratory workers in Maryland. They had caught brucellosis by working with it in connection with studies our government was doing on bacterial warfare! Yet, in an official report, they were told they could not use chronic disease as an excuse not to work.

Alice felt great empathy toward these 16 employees, and followed the case avidly. She had the time and the indignation. When she realized no one was coming to the lab workers' defense, she wrote to the top man – the Surgeon General of the United States. She pointed out that the official evidence was faulty and "...pleaded for further investigations to find a reliable method to detect chronic brucellosis." The Surgeon General, she said, accepted her suggestions in good grace and promised that efforts would be made to remove any stigma from the unfortunate patients.

Back in the 1930's, Alice recalled, undulant fever was so common that, after Dr. Walter Simpson's work in the Midwest, nearly everyone knew someone who suffered from brucellosis, diagnosed or undiagnosed. But as late as 1952, Simpson said that a "vast majority" of undulant fever cases went unrecognized in rural areas and cities where people still drank raw milk.

Mayo Clinic researchers in the '50's also issued a report, in a series, on brucellosis. They listed a dozen areas of the body where damage can localize, to become active years later. Tests taken during this time on infected tissue showed, amazingly, a negative response and "no physical findings could be attributed to the diseased organ." All of which Alice knew from her own experience. It was a ghost disease, hovering, hiding, waiting to rattle its chains of joint pain, fever and chills. No one knew brucellosis better than Alice. She could, sadly, claim this disease as her very own.

****

Alice could not have foreseen her popularity as a speaker, but after she left off reporting to the laboratory, her calendar began to fill with lecture engagements. The women's movement for equality now had a foothold, and if not a sturdy one, at least it was stable. Alice relished every opportunity to talk to women's groups on the subject of a female entering a male-dominated career. She did not rail against men, complain or make judgments. She researched the facts, put them in order and presented them.

When she stood before the Federation of Women's Clubs, the audience heard her commence with a series of mini-biographies. Life stories of women whose scientific contributions were so outstanding that historians had to record their attainments.

"...The reason that women's achievements are not

192

well known is because they do not receive the same recognition as those of men..." she began.

Continuing, "Women have proved that their mental capacity for scientific achievement is equal to that of men..." She warned listeners that a woman entering a scientific field likely would not get fair treatment. She went on to point out an unusual perception.

"...The woman who attains a highly specialized training and later makes no use of it is a hindrance to the progress of her sex. Men say that her educational opportunity should have gone to a man who would have made it a stepping stone to a successful career, and consequently, those who follow her find the restrictions to a woman's progress a little more severe..."

To those women who had firmly decided to pursue a career in science she advised not to get an advanced college degree without first working in their chosen field. Actual experience, Alice said, would allow a woman to "know herself better" and to find out if she really wanted a career.

Alice mentioned microscopic sciences as being more friendly to women than older sciences. We can see her fleeting smile as she said, "...Devotion to minute details in quiet seclusion does not appeal to most men."

Ever stout-hearted, Alice remained in the Washington, D.C. area, living the good life, slowed only a little by old age.

"Sally" Branham lived to be 80 and died in 1968. Sara had spent the last ten years of her life, after retiring as chief of the bacterial toxins section of N.I.H., promoting science education about meningitis.

Alice, along with several of her women colleagues, had been active for decades in the American Association of

University Women. The September, 1975, N.I.H. RECORD reported that Alice "never lost interest in young people and education; in 1969 she established a scholarship fund for the Federal City College. The gift was made through the American Association of University Women."

Alice C. Cole, who, at one time was president of A.A.U.W. in Washington, remembers that she worked with our Alice on a project or two. About Evans' move to Goodwin House, a retirement home in Alexandria, Virginia, Miss Cole said "...she had a studio-type room. I don't think she was very comfortable with this change..."

Shortly after Alice gave up her small apartment, Morgan died of kidney problems. He was 93 years old and had lost Zoe a few months before. They had held off going to an Ohio nursing home until the last 4 years, and Morgan's mind was alert until the end.

Alice was to have six years as part of the Goodwin community of oldsters. A year after she entered the retirement home, 1970, she was elected to the prestigious National Academy of Science.

Miss Cole, when she heard that Alice had fallen very ill and was in a hospital section of the home, visited her.

"...She knew me, but was not in good shape, and died soon thereafter..."

On September 5, a stroke took Alice from her earthly place, a place that had alternately rejected and embraced her. Her remains were returned to Neath and buried in the family plot, next to her mother and father and the tiny, unnamed infant girl, dated 1878.

Alice's marker is a rectangle of marble. It reads,

ALICE C. EVANS
1881-1975

The gentle hunter, having pursued and tamed her quarry, crossed over to a new home.

Her own words, written a decade before her death in the epilogue of her <u>Memoirs</u>, remind readers that her then 20 years of retirement gave a "...point of vantage to review with considerable objectivity the events that shaped my career..."

Continuing she wrote, "...Certainly, there are regrets over difficult situations that might have been handled better. But the course that was open for my ship to sail was, on the whole, gratifying..."

The world, especially Alice's beloved United States, is indeed gratified and indebted to her for the distinctive, courageous contribution she made to medical science. Largely because of Alice's efforts, pasteurization laws were passed in this country. All state governments, between the years 1964-67 voted to adhere to an amendment of the Federal Pasteurized Milk Ordinance - Act # 233 - requiring commercial milk to be pasteurized.

..."The going was rough at times, and there were stretches of clear sailing, too," Alice wrote, ending her autobiography.

On that smooth water, Alice departed this world. The course she had chosen to navigate touched the lives and well-being of millions of persons during her lifetime, and countless others beyond.

END

CHRONOLOGY

Alice Catherine Evans

(1881-1975)

1917 .... "twin microbes."

Read paper on dangers of raw milk to Society
1917 .... of American Bacteriologists

This report was published in <u>The Journal of</u>
1918 .... <u>Infectious Diseases</u>

Transferred to Hygienic Laboratory
Wash., D.C., as an
1918 .... Associate Bacteriologist

Worked on World War I
research, concentrating on
1918 .... influenza and meningitis

Dr. Theobald Smith disputed her
theory that brucellosis
1918 .... can be transmitted from animal to humans

Became infected with goat strain of the
1922 .... <u>brucella</u> microbe

Hospitalized with undulant fever
for 10 weeks. Her paper on the
<u>abortus</u> organism was read by a
1922 .... colleague at the World Dairy Congress

Dr. Charles Carpenter of
New York vigorously took
1925 .... up her <u>brucella</u> cause

Spoke on the dangers of
brucellosis to the American
1925 .... Society of Tropical Medicine

1926 .... Appointed to National
Research Council. Served 6 years

Became first woman president of the Society of
1928 .... American Bacteriologists
1928 .... Continued work in meningitis research
1929 .... Again hospitalized with undulant fever

	Milk pasteurization laws are being passed
1930	in most of America's large cities
	Dr. Walter Simpson of Ohio validated her
1930	brucella research
	Delegate to First International Congress
1930	of Microbiology, Paris, France
	Researched therapeutic
	antiserum for streptococcus
1930	bacillus
	Studied streptococci at National Institute
1932	for Medical Research, London, England
	Received Honorary Doctor of Medicine Degree
	Women's Medical School,
1934	Pennsylvania State College
	Received Honorary Doctor of Science Degree,
1936	Wilson College, Chambersburg, PA
1939	Ceased brucella research
1939-1945	Continued work in streptococci
	Chosen as "Outstanding Woman" by Woman's
1940	Centennial Congress
	Retired. Honored at joint
1945	retirement party with Ida Bengtson.
	Served as President of Committee on Brucellosis
1946	Mexico City, Mexico
	Continued to represent Inter
	American Congress on Brucellosis
	Received honorary Doctor of Science Degree,
1948	University of Wisconsin
	Was delegate at expert panel of the Third
1950	IACOB
	Lived independently. Spoke and lectured

198

1950-1966 ....for women's right to a career
1966 ....Moved to Goodwin House,
                                    Alexandria, Virginia
Sept. 5, 1975 ....Died of a stroke, age 94

Bibliographical Notes

The foundation for this narrative is Alice's autobiography, <u>Memoirs</u> which she wrote, at 82 years of age, in response to a request from **Dr. Wyndam Miles**, Historian of the National Institutes of Health. True to form, she specified where the first eight copies were to be placed.

<u>Memoirs</u> is a remarkable work attesting to her superb retentive memory and writing skill. My copy originated at the National Library of Medicine in Bethesda, Maryland.

When you find a quotation in the story with no source indicated, it will be from <u>Memoirs</u>.

References are listed in the approximate order in which the subject matter is found in the story.

The description of **Susquehana Collegiate Institute** was taken from L.H. Everts & Co., <u>The History of Bradford County</u>, Philadelphia, 1878, pp. 342. For **historical background** I went to the booklet by Edward Hartmann, <u>The Welsh of Wilkes-Barre and Wyoming Valley</u>, St. David's Society of Wyoming Valley, Inc., 1885, pp. 7-11. Also helpful was <u>The Harvard Encyclopedia of American Ethnic Groups</u>, Belknap Press, 1981, pp. 1012-1014; <u>The Annals of America</u>, Encyclopedia Britannica, 1968, Vol. 10, pp. 493, 504, supplied other background material. The Bradford County Historical Society, Towanda, Pa., provided Alice's **"Centennial" letter.** Certain details about the **Evans and Howell families** came from Alice herself in a recorded interview, 1956, and Dr. Elizabeth O'Hern's <u>Profiles of Pioneer Women Scientists</u>, Acropolis Books Ltd., Wash. DC. 1986, p. 128.

Some information on **Alice's childhood** and **high**

school days came from the 1956 taped interview. The description of **an early school** is from an illustrated history by L.H. Everts and Co., <u>The History of Bradford County</u>, Philadelphia, 1878, p. 342. **Carl Sandburg's autobiography,** <u>Always The Young Strangers,</u> Harcourt & Brace, NY, 1953, pp. 220-222, is Alice's source used in retelling Sandburg's family tragedy.

Biographical material on **Liberty Hyde Bailey** was culled from an article by Norris Ingells, "The Adventures of Liberty Hyde Bailey", <u>The Lansing State Journal</u>, Mar. 11, 1992. More facts came from <u>The 4-H Story</u>, a publication from the Iowa State University Press, 1951.

Dr. Robert Koch's biographical facts, here and in Chapter 8 came from <u>World Book Encyclopedia</u>, Vol. 10, 1963, p. 287, and those about the **compound microscope**, Vol. 12, pp. 426. Other data about the **simple microscope** I took from Brian Ford's, <u>Single Lens: The Story of the Simple Microscope, Harper & Rowe, New York, 1975, p. 19.</u>

Facts about **Dr. Elmer McCollum** came mostly from Alice's autobiography; certain information about vitamins I got from <u>World Book Encyclopedia</u>, 1989, Vol. 13, p. 334.

The four papers Alice published with **Prof. Hastings, and/or Dr. E.B. Hart** are listed in her <u>Memoirs,</u> p. 95.

Quotations of **Paul de Kruif** are from his long article, "Before You Drink A Glass of Milk", <u>Ladies' Home Journal</u>, Sept., 1929. The fateful "twin microbe" dramatization was based on de Kruif's magazine article. Some descriptions of de Kruif came from recollections of **Bill Gebhard** and **William Ferguson,** bacteriologists from Lansing, Michigan, who were acquainted with Paul de Kruif.

Fragments of information about **eisteddfod** traditions I took from Hartmann's, The Welsh of Wilkes-Barre and Wyoming Valley. **Gwilym Gwent** specifics are from the Harvard Encyclopedia of American Ethnic Groups, Harvard University Press, Cambridge, 1981, p. 1016 and from Magda's pamphlet, The Welsh in Pennsylvania, p. 4.

Highlights of **Dr. David Bruce and wife, Mary**, are from de Kruif's book, The Microbe Hunters, Harcourt, Brace & World, Inc., N.Y., 1926. pp. 252-277, Harry F. Dowling's book, Fighting Infection; Conquest of the Twentieth Century, Harvard University Press, Cambridge, Massachusetts, 1977, p. 178 and the book, Brucellosis: Clinical and Laboratory Aspects, Young & Corbel, CRC Press, Boca Raton, FL, 1989, pp. 12, 13, 14. The philanthropic work of **Nathan Straus** is taken from Encyclopedia Britannica, Vol. 11, 1991, pp. 307-08.

Theobald Smith's brief life-story came from The Dictionary of Scientific Biography, Scribner and Sons, N.Y., 1980. pp. 480-81. **Evans** and **Wachter family history** I took from letters written by **Sarah J. Wachter** of Cuyahoga Falls, Ohio, Alice's niece.

Morgan Evans' marriage and other history came from Cornell University Alumni Biographical Information sheets he sent in Aug., 1937, to the university in Ithaca, N.Y.

Copies of **letters quoted** herein (except the Centennial Celebration letter,) I obtained from The Dept. of Manuscripts and University Archives, Cornell University Libraries, Ithaca, N.Y.

For describing **Dr. James Leake's work**, in addition to Alice's description of him, I used Public Health Service Bulletin # 752, p. 50. **Dr. Goldberger's study** of Pellagra is also outlined in this bulletin, pp. 34-38.

Some biographical facts about **Dr. Sarah Branham** and **Dr. Thomas Parran** came from the book, <u>Modern Miracle Men</u> by J.D. Ratcliff, Dodd, Mead & Company, N.Y. 1939, pp. 157-63 and pp. 179-83. Other **Branham** information was taken from Elizabeth O'Hern's, "Women Scientists in Microbiology" <u>Bioscience</u>, Vol. 23, No. 9, (Sept., 1973) pp. 539 and a sketch from the Biographical files on the History of Women in America in Schlesinger Library at Radcliffe College, Cambridge, MA.

Data about **Dr. George McCoy** and **Dr. Eloise Cram** I found in Margaret Rossiter's, <u>Women Scientists in America</u>, The Johns Hopkins University Press, Baltimore, 1982, pp. 230-34. Also, **Dr. Leon Jacobs**, who worked at the National Institute of Allergy and Infectious Diseases, wrote about **Eloise Cram** (they were colleagues) in his chapter, "Significant Contributions from the Division of Zoology and Its Successor Laboratories at the N.I.H., 1902-1970", printed by the Public Health Service in its publication <u>Intramural Contributions, 1887-1987</u>, in October, 1987. Details about the working lives of Doctors **McCoy** and **Goldberger** came from Bess Furman's <u>A Profile of the United States Public Health Service, 1798-1948</u> (Washington, D.C., Government Printing Office, DHEW Publication No. (NIH) 73-369).

"The New Germ Theory" data and some **Rocky Mountain spotted fever** information is from <u>Rocky Mountain Spotted Fever: History of a Twentieth-Century Disease</u> by Victoria A. Harden, Johns Hopkins University Press, Baltimore, MD, 1990, pp. 1-7.

The discussion of **brucellosis medication** is taken from <u>Current Medical Diagnosis and Treatment</u> by

Schroeder, Krupp, Tierney, and McPhee; Appleton & Lange, E. Nowalk, CT, 1991, 30th Ed., p. 994. and Harvey's Principles of Internal Medicine by Braunwald, McGraw-Hill, N.Y. 1987, pp. 611-12. **Buffalo** facts came from the Scottsbluff, NE, Star Herald April 9, 1991, in an article entitled, "Three Bison Die Before Judge Halts Kill." I thank **Dr. Norman Gatzemeyer**, Supervisor of the Brucellosis Serology Laboratory, State of Michigan, for clarifying for me the process of brucellosis detection in cattle.

Historical facts about the **Lubeck Tragedy** came from editorials in The American Journal of Public Health, Vol. 20, 1930, pages 1122-23 and Vol. 22, 1932, pp. 296-7.

Bonus Army data was taken from an article by Malcolm Cowley, "The Flight of the Bonus Army", New Republic, Aug. 17, 1932, as found in the Annals of America: Great Issues in American Life, Encyclopedia Brittanica, Inc., 1968, Vol. 15, pp. 148-152.

Dr. I. Forest Huddleson's Brucella Infections in Animals and Man, The Oxford University Press, N.Y., 1934, indicates in the bibliography that the author used Alice's abortus and melitensis papers from the years 1915, 1918, and 1923-24-25. This book revealed an exciting frontispiece photograph of the **Mediterranean Fever Commission** (a branch of the Royal Society of Tropical Medicine) taken in 1904, enabling me to study **Dr. David Bruce's** likeness. The description of Dr. Huddleson is taken from an interview of **Dr. William Ferguson** of Lansing, Michigan, and **Dr. Lucile Portwood** of Okemos, Michigan, one of a few women who worked at Michigan State College laboratories with Huddleson in 1941-42. She also furnished a description of the sounds, smells and feel of those early labs.

Dr. Margaret Pittman generously provided me with photographs and facts about National Institutes of Health notables. Her biography is from the periodical, <u>Annual Review of Microbiology</u>; the article, "A Life With Biological Products" 1990., Vol. 44, pp. 1-10, of which she is author.

Facts about the beginning of the **Hygienic Laboratory** and the eventual **National Institutes of Health** are taken from Encyclopedia Britannica, <u>Medical and Health Annual</u>; "Celebrating 100 Years of Medical Progress", Victoria A. Harden, Ph.D., 1989, pp. 158-175.

Mention of **Kekule's** closed carbon ring is from the book edited by Carl Jung, <u>Man and His Symbols</u>; Dell Books, N.Y., 1964, p. 27. The article by Milton Bracker, announcing an **undulant fever cure**, and dateline Mexico City is from the <u>New York Times</u>, Nov. 3, 1946.

Alice's tiff with **Medicare** officials came from <u>Notable American Women - The Modern Period</u>, edited by Sicherman, Green, Kantrov and Walker, Harvard University Press, 1980, Vol. 4, p. 220. Several newspapers noted **Alice's death** with biographies of her career: <u>The Washington Post</u>, Sept. 8, 1975, <u>The New York Times</u>, Sept. 9;, <u>The Washington Sun</u>, Sept. 9.

Index

208